Horror on Holiday
13 Tales of Terror

Jolene Wightman

Illustrations by SF Varney

Published by Metal Lunchbox Publishing
5257 Buckeystown Pike #508
Frederick, Maryland 21704

ISBN:978-1-7335118-2-7

DEDICATION

To my mother, who always knew I had it in me, and to Tom, who never let me quit.

CONTENTS

ACKNOWLEDGMENTS

For her many years of boundless words of comfort and support, I would like to thank my mother very deeply. She's the best mom and taught me to appreciate all things spooky! Thank you for always listening!

For his vast knowledge of all things occult and his unique view of the world, I thank my forever friend Tom Burns. He's one of a kind, and always there for me! This book, and many things in my life, would not have been possible without you.

For his insightful feedback, gracious humor, and calming presence in my life, I thank my good friend and fellow writer John-Paul Checkett. You're one of the only people I go to for advice, and yes, even for critique--which is really saying something!

Last but not least, this book would not have been possible without the kind encouragement of my friend, Ellen Lewis. Ellen is not only an eagle-eyed editor, she has made the entire process of a first publication a wonderful experience! It's been so great to work with you and Metal Lunchbox Publishing!

The Resolution: A New Year's Tale

Colleen chewed on the end of her straw. "Don't you just hate her?"

Ruby followed her co-worker's gaze across the company cafeteria. She spotted Alicia Ferguson tossing her gleaming hair and piling a green salad onto her tray. At least, she spotted three-quarters of Alicia Ferguson.

"I wonder what she's doing to lose so much weight that quickly." Ruby sighed. "I'd have to cut off an arm to lose ten pounds in a week. It's been a week, right? Has it even been a week?"

"More or less." Colleen continued to assess. "I mean, it's not just that though, right? Like, look at her skin." She pointed toward Alicia with her mangled straw. "Do you remember the Halloween party? The zombie makeup she wore?"

Ruby saw where this was headed. She pushed Colleen's straw-wielding hand down towards the table. "Yeah. I remember."

"No, really though," Colleen tossed the straw onto her tray, next to the wreckage of no less than eight ketchup packets. "She didn't even need makeup. She was just, already, bleh." Colleen dragged her fingers down her cheeks to demonstrate. "And now look at her. She's freakin' glowing." Colleen sighed. "You think she's had work done? Botox? Is that even a thing anymore?" She shook her head. "How can she afford it?"

"Maybe she's in love." Ruby gestured at the air around her. "Maybe she's living on love, sucking in the love-oxygen for sustenance. I don't know, but...I mean, shouldn't we be happy for her?"

Colleen laughed. "Hell no! When I'm in love, I get new-boyfriend fat. I do nothing but go out to dinner and feel good about my chubby body. Who does she think she is, getting so skinny? Christmas was last week. She should have at least another month of stretchy pants to go...You gonna finish that, sweetie?"

"Yeah. Well. No. Here." Ruby handed over the rest of her chicken strips.

"Anyway." Colleen crunched down. "We shoulf asv her." Gulp. "Awe, damn, I'm out of ketchup."

"Ask and ye shall receive, children."

Ketchup packets rained down from the heavens and landed on Ruby's tray. She looked up to catch a boyish grin eclipse the fluorescent light.

"None for me, Nathan." Ruby began to pile the packets onto Colleen's tray. "This lady here, she's the one single-handedly depleting the east coast of tomato products."

Nathan sat down next to Ruby.

"Tomato, to-mah-to."

Colleen stopped chewing. "One more like that and you're banished from the cool kids' table."

"Y'know, Colleen, from where I'm sitting, that's the cool kids' table." Nathan nodded toward the other end of the cafeteria, where Alicia was chatting with the director of marketing.

"Hot damn. Look who's moving up in the world." Colleen said flatly.

"Yeah, but Alicia's always been so quiet. I asked to borrow a marker once and she just tossed the box over my cube wall," remarked Ruby. "Hit me right on the head. She's not super talkative. Maybe we should check on her or something."

"Okay. I'll get right on that," Colleen squeezed a blob of red goo onto her tray.

"What do you expect, Rubes?" asked Nathan. "It's New Year's. Maybe her resolution was to lose weight, fix her skin, chat up management, and rapidly move up the ranks of our fair company."

"Hm. Maybe."

"If you're worried, why not just ask her how she's doing? She's probably on some juice cleanse detox and will try to sell you a few gallons," sighed Nathan.

"Right." Colleen jabbed a fry in Ruby's direction. "Do not–I repeat–do not, let her sell you on a pyramid scheme. Because I am not buying crap from you. Just so you know."

"Of course you won't," Ruby snagged the fry from Colleen's hand and popped it in her mouth. "You haven't even paid me back for that movie ticket the other night."

"Your payment was the pleasure of my company," Colleen retorted.

"Then I demand a full refund. I'd like to speak with your supervisor."

Nathan cut in warmly, "So nice that I can be here for your lovers' quarrels."

"Nathan's just jealous because he doesn't have a work wife, too," sniped Colleen. Ruby laughed.

"No. You're right, I don't." Nathan admitted. "But you never know. I might have one soon."

For the second time that day, Ruby traced a friend's stare to three-quarters of Alicia Ferguson. For the first time that day, it bothered her.

. . .

After three trips by Alicia's cubicle, Ruby became desperate and dropped a pen. The pen bounced silently into the bland, beige box that stored her new and improved co-worker. Ruby wondered why she didn't just walk up to Alicia and say, 'Hey, looking good! What's your secret?Bathing in the blood of virgins?'

The truth was, Ruby felt...intimidated.

"Oh, hey Alicia. Dropped my pen!" Ruby laughed

Alicia beamed a huge, gleaming, white smile in Ruby's direction. "Ruby! How are you? You look great!"

"Oh, me? I do? Thank you! To be honest...I've been meaning to tell you how good you look."

"Stop, you're sweet," grinned Alicia.

"No I mean it.You look really pretty. Did you dye your hair?"

"So nice of you to ask. No, I didn't!" More smiling.

"Oh, sorry, it just...looks lighter or something. And I don't mean to be rude by asking, but, you lost some weight, right?"

Alicia continued to bare her teeth at Ruby, in the friendliest way possible.

"You know Ruby, I did lose some weight!"

"I could definitely tell! Mind sharing your secret?"

Alicia's smile went on a little too long. Didn't her cheeks hurt yet?

"What makes you think that I have a secret, Ruby?"

Ruby cocked her head. "No, I don't I guess, I...It's just, you seem different lately."

Alicia's effervescent smile ticked down a notch.

"I'm sorry," babbled Ruby. "I'll leave you to it."

A few swift steps and Ruby was tucked into her own cubicle. "Urgh, idiot," she sighed as she sank into her chair.

Ruby's muttering was interrupted by a short 'psst.' She looked up to see Alicia's blonde head hovering over the top of the wall. "Your pen," she chirped merrily.

"Oh, right, thanks," Ruby reached up for her pen.

"And also..." Alicia handed down a white business card.

Ruby turned it over. The black letters read, "The New You: Transformation of Mind, Body and Soul."

"Now it's our little secret," Alicia winked, and then she dropped out of sight.

. . .

"Oh gross! It is a pyramid scheme!" Colleen tossed the card down on the table as if it were diseased.

"We don't actually know that, Colleen." Ruby scooped up a spoon of mac and cheese.

"We don't? Nathan,do we not know it's a pyramid scheme?"

Nathan shrugged. "I guess we don't know for sure."

Colleen gasped. "Et tu, Brute?"

Ruby rolled her eyes. "Would you feel better if I promise not to give them my email address?"

"Who cares? It's my email I'm worried about. Promise you won't share it, I get enough junk mail." Colleen drew a triangle in the air with two fingers while mouthing, 'pyramid scheme.'

"I have to say," said Nathan between sips of iced tea, "if that's a scheme, it's a pretty good one."

Ruby shook her head, "Hm?"

Nathan gestured toward Alicia with his fork. "Whatever she's doing, it's working."

Ruby eyed Alicia across the cafeteria. Within the span of a few weeks she had blossomed from plain to extraordinary. She sighed and set down her spoon.

"Looks like it." Ruby looked at Nathan. Nathan looked at Alicia.

And Colleen watched them both with curiosity.

...

"You look nervous."

The man sitting across from Ruby was something out of a 1950s film: handsome in a generic, slick-haired, white-toothed sort of way. "I guess I am. I don't know why," she admitted.

The man laughed. "Don't be! That just shows me that you're serious about becoming 'The New You!' I like that sort of commitment."

"Yes, well…" Ruby looked around. The New You's central office was located in a posh building downtown. She had been welcomed by a stylish secretary into a sleek black-and-white lounge that this man insisted was an office. "I just wanted to check it out, I guess."

The man stuck out his hand, "Name's Hank. Good to meet you, Ruby."

Ruby took his hand. It was oddly cold. He gave it two firm shakes before releasing her.

"Alicia told me you might come by. She said you were curious about her results with our program."

"Yes, she…" Ruby cleared her throat. "She looks so happy lately."

Hank snapped, clapped and pointed finger-guns at her chest. "And that is the secret. It's not about weight loss, or beautiful hair and skin. It's about

4

a total transformation of mind, body, and soul. That's what some people don't understand. You can't change the outer you without changing the inner you."

Ruby considered his pitch for a moment. "And what does the program entail? Alicia didn't give me any details."

"Ah, she wouldn't. It's simple, yet profound. She could tell you the steps, but you'd miss the essence of the program." Hank smiled like the living headshot that he was. "Also, there is the matter of the non-disclosure policy."

She was taken aback. "Non-disclosure? Why?"

Hank waved his hand to dismiss the question. "We can't give away our trade secrets now, can we? We have to keep the bills paid! The New You also keeps its eye out for the right sort of client. We like to choose people we know will succeed. And I do believe that is you!"

This stranger's confidence in her left Ruby uneasy. "Okay, but…what would I have to do?"

"Before we go into the details, Ruby, I just need to ask. Why is it that you've come here today? What is it that you want out of your transformation to your best self?"

'Ask and ye shall receive, children!'

"Um," Ruby started. "It's really because…" She considered the man before her, started again, "I suppose I… want to be the best me that I can be."

Hank's grin widened, if that were even possible.

"Perfect."

…

Ruby started her New You transformation the following morning.

It seemed easy enough. She was to take one capsule of proprietary blend, non-stimulating, organically gathered vitamins and essential nutrients at breakfast. Before bed, she was to hold her Change Token: a smooth, green, heart-shaped stone that shone holographic in sunlight and seemed perpetually warm. While holding the token, she was to recite an inspirational phrase.

"I am what I become, and in becoming, I am me."

Finally, she was to meet with her coach once a week. Hank was right-- it was all a little too simple. They didn't even charge her for it, other than an initial $20 paperwork fee.

Of course, there was one other detail…

'Ah, Ruby, before you go, one thing to stress… It seems strange, I know, but it is essentialthat you follow this rule to the letter. During the course of your program, you should avoid looking into mirrors. Now, feel free to use your rear view, of course, we don't want to cause an accident…' he laughed, 'but I strongly advise you avoid looking at your reflection during this process. We find that it delays the results. After all, it's difficult to transform into your best self while still clinging to the old one!'

Ruby wasn't sure how she'd manage to follow this rule. Still, Alicia must be following it, at least to some extent, and her transformation was extraordinary. Ruby was determined to adhere to this program to the letter. She brushed her teeth at the kitchen sink, ran a comb through her hair, and patted on some cream blush on her cheeks, all the while hoping for the best.

When Ruby arrived at work that morning, she found Alicia waiting for her at her desk.

"Ah, there she is! Congratulations, Ruby. Here's to the first day of the rest of your life!" Alicia offered Ruby a small chocolate cupcake.

"Oh, thanks Alicia, that's sweet of you," Ruby said. "Hey, I'm glad you're here. I wanted to ask you about…the whole mirror thing? I mean, do you really do that?"

Alicia's smile stretched ear to ear. "Of course," she chirped.

"Okay but, isn't that hard? I mean, how do you avoid all mir—"

"Ah, Ruby, remember," and now Alicia whispered, "non-disclosure. Someone might overhear. If you have questions, please ask your coach. Anyway!" Alicia was halfway out of the cube when she said, "Have a wonderful day!"

"Yeah…you too…" Ruby watched Alicia float away. Well, at least she'd gotten a cupcake out of the interaction.

…

Three days into the program, and Ruby had followed each and every step in its fullest detail. Despite much difficulty and temptation, she had even managed to avoid all mirrors. It wasn't easy. Her results were well worth the effort: Ruby had lost a pants size, she felt full of energy, and her hair felt silkier. Whatever this magic was, she didn't want it to wear off. Nathan had even noticed.

'Looking good today, Rubes!'

Ruby beamed as she shopped for a few necessities at the dollar store. At this rate, she'd be a knock-out by Valentine's Day. She already pictured sitting down to an elegant dinner, and not alone this time.

Ruby finally decided between two scents of hand soap. She plunked the chosen bottle into her basket and looked up. In a moment of carelessness, her eyes moved past the security mirror located in the corner of the store.

There, in the reflection, she saw it.

She spotted herself, of course, and was pleased at the slimmer, sunnier Ruby that stood in the personal care aisle. But there was more.

It was only for a moment, and almost out of view. But there, in the back of the store, stood someone… something…

It looked like her, but…it wasn't. It was a woman, Ruby's height, same build, same dark hair, but...

Ruby turned away. She wasn't supposed to look into mirrors! She had already, though, so what was the harm in one more peek?

It was closer this time, as if it had traveled three feet in a single second. The woman– thing?–was bent forward at the waist. Its hair hung, limp and tangled, toward the floor. Its arms dangled long and lifeless. It was wearing a simple white dress, but it appeared soiled, faded, as if decades old.

Ruby's heart raced. She spun around.

Nothing was there.

Gathering whatever composure and self-control she had left, Ruby dropped her basket and rushed out of the store.

…

"I see you're progressing well! Look at you." Ruby's coach, Lana, had the same overbearing smile and too-white teeth as the rest of the 'New You's.'

"Yes, I lost six pounds," nodded Ruby.

"Wonderful! And your skin is so clear. You're glowing!"

"Thank you," replied Ruby as she sipped a glass of water.

"Any challenges we should talk about?" asked Lana.

"Not really, it's been pretty easy so far. Most of it, anyway."

Lana leaned forward and topped off Ruby's glass.

"Ruby, we've all been through the program. You can be honest with me."

"Well…it's just that...that mirror rule."

"Ah yes," smiled Lana. "We've all struggled with that rule!"

"You have?" questioned Ruby.

"Ofcourse! We're all so used to staring at ourselves all the time. How narcissistic!" She laughed. "But remember that focusing on the superficial distracts us from the real change–the one inside of us." Lana held a hand over her heart.

"Right. Yeah, I can see that for sure, but…"

Lana held Ruby in her beautiful, green-eyed stare.

"Ruby," Lana leaned in confidentially, "you looked into a mirror, didn't you? … It's okay! We all slip at the beginning. The main thing is to keep trying. You'll get there!"

Ruby wrestled with her next question. "When you looked into the mirror, did you…see anything?"

"Hm?" asked Lana. She squeezed a wedge of lemon into her water.

"I mean, did you see anything unusual?"

Lana's green eyes landed on Ruby's face.

"I did, yes."

Ruby was a little afraid of her answer, but I had to ask. "What did you see?"

"Okay Ruby, I'll level with you. The truth is, some people report experiencing mild visual hallucinations during early stages of the program."

"Oh." Ruby blinked. "I feel like I should have been warned about this."

"Well think about it. If we told you, you might be less willing to sign up. And look at how far you've come already."

Ruby sipped her water. Lana's strangely cold hand dropped onto her knee. "Listen," she said, "Whatever you saw, it was probably just a strange side effect of our proprietary herb blend. For some reason it always seems worse when looking into a mirror. Our staff has been working on this, but it shouldn't deter you from your progress."

Ruby shook her head, "I don't know if I'd call this a 'mild' hallucination…it was…"

"Oh relax, Ruby! It's perfectly normal to feel like you do at this early stage. But stick with it! Don't forget your daily affirmation with the Change Token. Drink plenty of water, take your tablets. Before you know it, you'll be a new woman!"

Ruby nodded, "Yeah." She brightened, "I do feel better. More energy, you know?"

Lana beamed. "And you'll keep right on feeling better! As long as you dodge those pesky mirrors."

...

Nathan had been staring at her, discreetly, for the entire elevator ride.

With some careful planning, Ruby had followed the program for a solid three weeks. Her figure was whittling, her hair like silk. Despite not being able to view her reflection, Ruby knew without a doubt that she looked beautiful. She felt fresh, light, and luminous. She had purchased a new wardrobe and tossed her makeup. Who needed it? She was indeed becoming a new woman .

It appeared that Nathan had noticed, too. Nathan was usually quick to make small talk. Not so much these days.

Ruby threw a blinding smile at him, reveling in the way it made him shift nervously. She was getting good at this now. It was becoming easy.

"Um, hey Rubes!"

"Nathan!"

"Colleen's been missing you at our loser lunch table."

"Oh, I know, it's a shame. Now that I'm promoted to lead help desk, I have a different schedule!" "Yeah. Right...Congratulations, by the way," he grinned. "That's really awesome. Didn't know you were going for that."

Ruby shrugged breezily. "I wasn't! It just sort of happened." She chirped,

"I miss you two. Lunch isn't the same without the ketchup piles!"

"We miss you too. I mean, at least I do," he chuckled.

"Get your story straight, buddy! Is it you, or is it Colleen who's been crying into your milk cartons?" she jabbed.

With a ding! the elevator opened. Nathan turned and looked at her, square in the eye. He searched her face, appearing to study her. After a moment, he stepped out.

"I guess it's both of us. Hey, we should meet up for drinks sometime. You in?"

Ruby smirked. "I'll check my schedule and get back to you."

The door closed. Ruby tossed her head back in delight. "Yes!" She reveled in the feeling. In her bliss, she squeezed her eyes shut and took a deep breath.

When she opened her eyes, they landed directly on the security mirror.

Before she knew what was happening, she saw it.

Once more it was doubled forward, like some macabre ragdoll. It stood several feet behind her. Its hair dangled towards the floor, filthy and unkempt. Its fingertips nearly touched its bare, dirty feet.

This time, Ruby couldn't look away. She stared at the thing for as long as she could bear it. Goosebumps rose on her arms, but she was transfixed.

The woman-creature was absolutely still-- no, there was movement. A worm twisted through its hair.

From behind her, a low, guttural voice began to croak,

"I am…what I…become…"

Ruby whipped around. Nothing was there. Her face was hot with streaming tears. She heard the elevator open behind her, and out she dashed.

…

"Y-you d-don't understand, it, it spoke, it–"

"Ruby."

"It did, it spoke and it's, it's, it's awful, please I–"

"Ruby!" Lana shouted from Ruby's cell phone. "Please. Calm down."

Ruby wiped her eyes with a tissue. "You didn't see it, you can't possibly understand what I'm–"

"Look, I get it. You should have seen what I saw during the early phase of the program. Listen to me! It's okay! It's just a side effect of the—"

"I know, the pills, but then maybe I should stop taking them!"

Lana sighed. "We lose too many people at this stage. Ruby, you worked so hard. Look at how far you've come. If you can just stick it out a bit longer, you'll be there. You'll be the woman you've always wanted to be."

"I don't know if I can," cried Ruby. "This thing is just, it's so horrible!"

9

"Horrible, yes. Real? No. Change is hard. Your mind will play tricks on you to keep you stuck. Transformation does not come easily for any of us. But if you're committed, you'll reach your goals." She sighed. "I know it's scary. Drink some tea, watch a movie. You'll feel better in the morning."

Ruby sniffled in response.

"And Ruby? You've got to be better about dodging those mirrors. You're almost at the end. Don't blow it now."

...

Six weeks into the program, and Ruby was resplendent. She swiveled every head that she crossed. She no longer needed coffee–or much sleep, for that matter. Ruby was lighter than air. She was transformed. She was energized, focused, and born anew.

Well, almost born anew, anyway.

Despite her considerable line of suitors, Ruby thought only of Nathan. He hadn't reached out since their interaction in the elevator. Ruby tried not to think of that event very often, marred as it was by the twisted being's horrific appearance.

When would he finally make his move? No matter. Ruby's final coaching session was scheduled for that evening. She had to set aside the feelings inspired by crushes and creatures and focus on completing the program.

Ruby's thoughts were interrupted by a familiar voice.

"There you are, you freakin' stranger."

Ruby looked up from her desk to see Colleen looming over her.

"Colleen!" She threw her a freshly-patented, gleaming smile.

"Cut the crap, Ruby."

Ruby faltered. "Uh–what?"

"I've been texting you for weeks. You move up two floors and we're dead to each other? What's the deal?"

"I'm sorry, I…"

"No you're not. You're happy as can be with your new friends and your freakish smile and your skinny body."

Ruby began to stand, "No, Colleen, please…I've been so busy with everything and–"

"Save it," Colleen snapped. "You know, I don't want to hang out with you anyway. I want to see my friend, Ruby. If you see her, ask her to give me a call." Colleen turned and began to march away. Several pairs of eyes followed her.

"Colleen…"

Ruby's friend turned and looked at her. She shook her head, and vanished around the corner.

Ruby collapsed at her desk. She rubbed her temples, smoothed her hair.

As she calmed herself, her phone buzzed. Ruby snapped it up, hopeful to see Colleen's name with a 'just kidding' attached to it.

No, not Colleen. It was Nathan. He'd sent a text.

"Do you have plans for Valentine's Day?"

Ruby bit her lip to keep from smiling. She took a moment and then responded. Joyfully, she typed her reply.

"I do now!"

...

Ruby donned her favorite dress for her last coaching session. She was in a mood to celebrate.

"You look stunning!" Lana threw her arms around Ruby in a hug when she arrived.

"Are you excited? You should be!" Hank boomed as he walked in the room behind Ruby.

"I am, yes! Thank you!"

"Well, if we're going to have a graduation ceremony, we should probably head to the ceremonial chamber!" Hank announced gleefully.

"The—what?" Ruby laughed with him.

"Oh, Hank is being dramatic," teased Lana.

Hank led them back through a hallway to a darkly varnished wooden door. It featured ornate scrollwork and was inlaid with the same green stones as the Change Token.

"The drama continues!" taunted Ruby.

Upon entering, Ruby spotted three chairs. Not chairs—thrones.

"Is this...for me?"

"Of course, Ruby! Please, sit."

They all sat down. Ruby glanced around the room. It was much bigger than she would have anticipated. It was also dim and windowless. The walls were covered in rich purple paper. On each wall there hung a painting, or she guessed it was a painting, covered in a black curtain. "I'm a little confused," she said.

"Ah, just pomp and circumstance," chuckled Hank. "Ruby, we are so proud of you. You have come so very far. Look at you! You really are transformed."

Ruby smiled. "Thank you. It wasn't that hard. I do feel different now. Like...I'm finally my best self."

"Wonderful," grinned Lana. "You're so close now. You're right on the brink of a new beginning."

"Oh?" Ruby looked between the two. She laughed. "I feel like I've already started my new life!"

Lana and Hank flashed their wide, toothy smiles.

11

"You've prepared yourself well. But your new life truly begins today."

"Well, great! So...is there a certificate, or..." Ruby looked around for something to sign, or perhaps a certificate to display at home.

Another round of laughter erupted from the grinning twins.

"Not quite, Ruby. Come over here, will you?"

Ruby stood and followed Lana to the largest of the covered paintings.

"You've done so well with the program. Most people really struggle. It's taken a lot of self-control, but things are going to be easier from here."

Ruby stared at the black velvet curtain. Unease crept over her.

Lana continued, "Ruby, are you ready to see the New You?"

"Wait…" she protested, "that's not a–"

With a short tug, Lana pulled back the curtain to reveal a gleaming, silver mirror.

The bent creature stood behind her, closer than ever.

"No!" shouted Ruby, spinning around. "I don't want to see that thing!"

As if on cue, Hank, positioned at the other end of the room, pulled back the next curtain.

Now it stood just feet behind her. Its hunched shoulders were lost in a tangled mat of dark hair. Beneath the dank tresses, Ruby caught a glimpse of skin.

It was rotting.

"Please, no!" Ruby ran for the exit. She stopped.

A full length mirror was anchored to the door.

"No…" Ruby shook her head.

The bent creature stood mere inches behind her now. Ruby could feel the chill from its skin, smell the decay of its flesh. Its hair crept along her arms like threads of a spiderweb. It began to speak in that same rattling husk of a voice.

"I am what I become…"

"No, please!" Ruby cried. Slowly, the creature rolled upright, uncoiling from its bent and broken position. It clutched a green stone in its putrid hand.

"… and in becoming, I am me."

. . .

"Cheese fondue for two?" The waiter set down plates of bread and vegetables, along with a pot of molten cheese.

"Yes, thank you." Nathan nodded. He was wearing a tweed jacket. His hair was styled. He was also sweating a little. "Rubes, I'm so glad you said yes to this. I mean, I've wanted to ask you out for a while now, but…"

Ruby beamed a perfectly pearlescent smile across the table.

"But?" she asked sweetly.

"But you've seemed pretty busy," he gestured toward the flawless vision that was Ruby, "improving yourself and all." He laughed, "Sorry, that didn't come out right."

"Don't worry, Nathan," she cooed. Ruby sipped her wine. "I know just what you mean. I do feel much improved."

"Ah, good…" He rubbed the back of his neck. "You look great, by the way."

"Nathan, you must remember one thing," she said softly.

Nathah appeared to be caught off guard. "And what's that?"

"True transformation does not occur from the outside in. It happens from the inside, out."

THE SHAWL: A VALENTINE'S TALE

Emma has been gone for two weeks now, but her mom's got a new silk shawl. She keeps wearing it when she picks up Emma's brother from school. It's pink. Sarah said it's pretty. I guess she's right about that. I don't really care.

It's been quiet at the playground. Less kids to play with lately. My best friend Sarah (that's the one I mentioned), she and I walk home together every day. We've been best friends since she moved here, I think that was last school year.

We always walk home together. I don't mind it because it's someone to talk to. But sometimes people give me a hard time about having a girl for a best friend. It's not so weird, boys and girls being friends.

Sarah got upset and started crying the other day. She said she misses Emma. I didn't know what to say, so I let her ride my bike. I don't usually let anyone ride my bike. I think she liked it.

We went to the park today and I brought my sidewalk chalk. We wanted Justin and Marcus to join, along with some of the other neighbor kids. When they didn't meet up with us, Sarah and I went to their door to ask their moms if they could come out.

Mrs. Donnelly smiled at us, funny, like she was hungry or something. But happy about it? I didn't like it. It made me feel weird, with butterflies in my stomach, like they say. Sarah didn't seem to like it much either, because she grabbed my hand.

I let Sarah hold my hand, but not because it's almost Valentine's Day. It's not like that. Once someone acted like it was like that, but I told him to shut up. And he was gone the next week, anyway. That one I wasn't so worried about. He was a jerk if I'm to be honest.

Anyway, Mrs. Donnelly kept touching her dress. A pink dress. Shiny, and it looked brand new. Sarah told her that she liked it. Mrs. Donnelly laughed when Sarah said this. I thought that was kind of mean. My mom is always on me about being "grateful" because "I don't know how much worse it could be." I do think it is nice to say thank you when someone says they like your dress. Not to laugh at them. But like I was saying, we asked about Justin and Marcus coming out to play. And Mrs. Donnelly said no, they were visiting their father in another state.

And Sarah said, "I thought their dad lived here."

And Mrs. Donnelly didn't say anything for a minute. But then she said, the boys are on a trip with their father, to another state."

But here's the thing. I heard a voice from the other room then, and it sounded like their dad.

And then Mrs. Donnelly closed the door.

…

Sometimes we play "Count the White Vans."

They showed up around Christmastime, but maybe sooner than that because we had a scarecrow in our yard still.

It's not really a fun game if I'm to be honest, because I don't really like the white vans. I don't know why. But there isn't much else to do right now, so I play too.

Sarah and I decided to make valentines for our friends. The teacher handed out a list of names but then she kept handing out new lists, with less names on them. Then she just started having us cross the names out. She said she was "wasting too much paper." I don't like doing that either. Crossing the names out, I mean.

The other night I got upset, and I will tell you, I did start to cry. I cried at dinner and I asked where Emma, Marcus, Justin, Luke, Jose, and Angela have all gone. My Mom and Dad, they told me that people sometimes move to a different area. But I see their parents, my friends' parents that is, and I just don't see my friends anymore. So I did get very worked up. I wanted my dad to hug me and he did.

But then he said something and it made me feel weird again, the butterflies in your stomach thing. He said, "I guess you should be happy you're still here with us!"

And then my mom laughed a little. Then they both kept eating their dinner.

I made sure to clean my room extra tidy that night. I've been keeping up with my chores really good this week. Mom and Dad haven't said anything about it.

…

Today was nice. Mom took Sarah and I to the amusement park. The lines were so short. I don't remember it being that way last year. Last year I got sunburn from waiting in line so long.

We had ice cream, funnel cake, and cheese fries. And my mom didn't want me to use my allowance money either. She said, "It's on me," and she kissed my head, which was embarrassing.

My mom wanted to take lots of pictures, which made it a little boring sometimes. I don't like stopping to pose. But Mom kept saying that she wants to remember this day. Sarah gave me bunny ears, I know it.

...

Sarah has been out sick from school for three days. I keep asking to go over, but Mom says no, she'll be back to school when she's ready.

But Sarah usually doesn't get sick for long. I asked Mom if we could mail her a card and she didn't answer me. I made Sarah a valentine too, but I'll save that for later. I can send her a get well soon card if Mom lets me. I just need a stamp. I hope she helps me. All Mom talks about these days is how much she wants a beautiful silk shawl of her own.

So I asked Dad for a stamp and he did this big loud sigh. I tried to give him a hug, and he said, "Asking for a lot, aren't we?" and kind of patted my head.

I've been in my room ever since.

...

Today I woke up early. One of those white vans is sitting outside of our house. They got here before the sun was even up, I bet.

They are sitting in the parking space in front of the yard, and the engine is running. I keep trying to see inside. There is a man in a white jacket, I think, and he reminds me of a milkman on old TV shows. He looks real friendly. I still wish he'd go away.

I'm feeling a little scared so I'm going downstairs. For some reason I think Sarah might be here. I don't know why. I would really like to see her.

But it's only Mom and Dad, and they're hugging each other. She just kissed his cheek. Mom looks really happy. So I ask them what's going on.

They both turn, and they reach their arms out for me. And they're smiling.

"Come here, son," they say, at the same time too.

I don't want to go over to them, but I do. I am scared and I wish Sarah was here. I want them to hug me. They put their arms around me, but tight—too tight. It hurts a little.

I look up, try to talk, and I want them to tell me that they love me.

But they just keep smiling.

THE HOLE: A ST PATRICK'S DAY TALE

Kelsie's dream of international travel always seemed to center around one destination: the bonnie green fields of Ireland.

A St. Patrick's Day travel deal popped up online, a little too conveniently, after she discussed her desire to travel with a friend one afternoon

"So much for privacy in my own home," she laughed.

Still, Kelsie soon clicked through image after image of lush rolling hills and moss-speckled cliffs. She imagined herself sitting in warm, golden pubs and sipping beer to live fiddle music. When she landed on the photo of a charming, white-and-red cottage wound with ivy, it was almost too much. A few calculations, a triple check of her bank account, and her trip was booked.

Time inched until it flew. Kelsie finally arrived in Ireland, fatigued and foggy from the flight. She was desperate to get settled into the cottage that would be her home for the next week. Her tour guide showed her around, motioning with one hand where Kelsie could toss down her luggage.

"Oh my gosh, I love it," Kelsie suddenly sprung back to life, buzzing from one end of the small cottage to the other. She marveled at the tiny kitchen, at the doilies adorning the painted wooden table. She picked up a petite, tin tea kettle and tapped its side with a fingernail. She rushed to the window to admire the view: a pristine emerald landscape save for the white sheep spotting the horizon. Everything was as it should be—the plank hardwood floors, the hand-woven rugs, the quilt-covered bed, the hole in the ceiling.

The hole in the ceiling?

Keslie blinked, turning her eyes toward the corner of the bedroom.

"Did you see that?" she asked her tour guide.

"See what, miss?"

"See the…" Keslie stared at nothing more or less than a perfect ceiling. She smiled. "Nothing. Thank you, Liam. It's really perfect."

"My pleasure," he grinned at Kelsie and ran a hand through his artfully disheveled brown hair.

Was *everything* this gorgeous in Ireland?

He went on, "I'll see you at the pub, then, if you're sure you've got what you need."

Mostly, thought Keslie, but she bid him farewell. Time to unpack. But maybe… a nap first.

Kelsie threw off her shoes, peeled back the blanket and buried herself in the cool bed. As her head dropped to the pillow, she saw it again, just from the corner of her eye.

A hole. A gaping, dark hole. In the ceiling.

Kelsie focused on the corner. It was gone. She waited for a moment, closed her eyes, and looked again.

"Maybe I'm going blind," Keslie said to no one in particular.

Within a few minutes, she was fast asleep.

…

Kelsie enjoyed a day of shopping, sight-seeing, and mild, hopeful flirtations with her handsome tour guide. There were other people in her group too, but Keslie reminded herself that there was no such thing as a perfect vacation. This, she admitted, was pretty close.

There was, of course, the issue of the ceiling. Kelsie tried to avoid looking at that area of the cottage, but found that only made things worse. When staring at something else, such as a picture on the wall or the wooden rocking chair, Kelsie could glimpse the spot in some fuzzy detail.

The hole had soft and irregular edges. Was it made of mold? It featured a dense blackness that was both discomforting and fascinating. Kelsie imagined what it would feel like to push her hand inside. Would it be cold? Wet? If she reached in, would something reach back? Kelsie shivered, repulsed yet enthralled by the idea.

Still, the very moment she focused on it, the hole would vanish as if it were never there in the first place.

"I'm losing it," Kelsie decided. She tried to move her thoughts away from the hole and its inky, unsettling allure.

This tactic worked well enough until Kelsie laid down for bed that night.Kelsie was well on her way to sleep when she first heard it.

It was…a baby's cry.

Kelsie jolted awake. Where had it come from? She looked wildly around the room.

"Hello?" she called, panicked.

Only silence answered.

One warm glass of milk later and Kelsie felt tentatively ready to try to sleep again. As she rested her head, she spotted the hole for just a moment.

Maybe she'd had too much to drink at dinner. But she was almost certain the baby's cry had come from there.

. . .

"Liam, would there be any other cottages available? Maybe I could trade?"

Liam was shoveling fries into his stubbled face. He looked at her for a moment before wiping his mouth with a napkin.

"I'm sorry, Kelsie, but none that I know of. I think we're full up. Is there something wrong with yours?"

Kelsie smiled. "No, it's fine, it's just…" She took a sip of her water. "I don't really know how to say this." She laughed, trying to find the words. She finally settled on, "I think there's a hole in my ceiling."

Liam placed his palms onto the thickly varnished table. "Is that all?" He flashed a smile while signaling for another beer. "Why don't we just patch that up for you then? Would that be all right?"

Kelsie shook her head. "No, I…I don't know why but…" She glanced around the table at the rest of her tour group. "I just, I really don't like it, I guess. Maybe I could trade or, maybe, I could find a hotel?" Kelsie stared at Liam, his beautiful gray eyes, his concerned brows. She went on, quietly, "The hole. It doesn't stay put. I look away and it's there, I look at it again and it's not."

It sounded even crazier out loud. Still, she went on.

"And I don't know for sure, but, I think, last night I heard…"

"Heard…what?" Liam's face suggested a deeper concern than Keslie cared for.

Kelsie tried to manage her most sane tone of voice.

"Liam, did anyone ever die in my cottage? Like maybe a baby or a child?"

At this Liam almost smiled, "Well yes, lots of people have died there over the years, I'm sure. Hate to say it." Liam leaned back, stretched his arms out wide over the booth back. "Sad as it is, kids have died all over the place around here. Famine will do that sort of thing. It's the less magical part of Irish history I suppose."

Kelsie looked around the table. A few more eyes were straying in her direction. Infant fatalities don't make for the best lunch conversation.

"Oh. Right." Kelsie picked up a fry. "I'm sorry. It's fine. I think I'm just tired."

Her heart kicked up a notch as Liam patted her arm.

"No worries at all, love. We'll make sure you get some rest. That's why you're on vacation, isn't it?"

. . .

Kelsie stared at the bed. Her teeth were brushed, pajamas on, feet slippered.

There was only one thing to do.

Kelsie, being slight of stature, struggled to shove the bed to the far end of the room. If nothing else, she would be at least ten feet away from the accursed, semi-visible hole. She had tried sleeping on the small couch but it was too firm, too short.

Kelsie settled in with her tea and her book. Only a few more days and she would be home…or a few more nights, anyway.

Kelsie teetered on the edge of sleep when the wailing started.

It was a soft sound, distant. But it was enough. Why was there a baby crying, and why was it crying in the corner of her ceiling?

Kelsie squeezed her eyes shut. It's not there, she reminded herself. "You're dreaming. Or you're tired. Or..."

Or maybe there really *was* a baby, and maybe it really *was* crying.

Kelsie felt sick as she approached the corner. She looked frantically around, her hands roaming the walls. "Hello!" she called. The hole blinked in and out of sight as the cries grew louder.

"Are you…" Kelsie shook her head, "Is there…is someone there?" Kelsie's pulse quickened as the pitiful wailing went on. Eventually, she steadied her nerves. She focused her gaze on the portion of the ceiling just outside of the hole.

From the blackness, so thick and solid, something moved.

Fingers. Tiny fingers curled around the edge of the hole, and the crying came to a sudden stop.

Kelsie could see the hole now. She could focus on it. She could stare straight into it.

Two tiny eyes stared back at her. They gleamed silver in the darkness.

And they looked hungry.

THE ANGEL: AN EASTER TALE

March 10th

Dear Diary,

I got my part in the Easter play! I was hoping for one of the Marys, but maybe next year.They say I'm too young still. At least I'm not a villager. I think Dad would have liked it if I'd gotten a big part...Oh well! At least I get a cool costume. I'm going to be an angel. (I don't remember there being an angel in last year's play.) Mrs. Arnold said that too many people want to be in it this year. So maybe that's why they're adding parts? Anyway, off to bed! Goodnight, Journal!

March 13th

Dear Diary,

I baked Dad some banana muffins. I thought they would cheer him up. He spends a lot of time in his room now. He said thanks but didn't eat one.

We had our first rehearsal last night. Being an angel is kind of boring. They did give me one line though. I think they're trying to be nice. We went out for ice cream after, so not a total loss.

I have a history test tomorrow. I almost went to the living room to ask Mom to study with me. It's really hard still. But they're letting me talk to the school counselor again after my test. Ms. M is awesome. She always makes me feel better.

Anyway I'm off to bed. Goodnight, Journal!

P.S. My back has been itching like crazy!!

March 15th

Dear Diary,

My back was so itchy that it woke me up last night. It's up on the shoulder blades. I can't stop scratching it. I went to the school nurse and she said I have two red spots back there, one on each side. She asked if she should call Mom or Dad to pick me up. Then the nurse got upset and said sorry a bunch of times. She said that she forgot. I'm a little jealous. Sometimes I wish I could forget, too. It might make the hurt go away.

We tried on our costumes tonight. They're just reusing the same old angel costume from the Christmas play. I kind of wish I could make my own or have a different one. This one makes me feel like a potato. In youth group we talked about the story of Jephthah and his daughter. I thought it was sad. I keep thinking about that poor girl and how she was sacrificed. Things like that give me nightmares.

Anyway, off to bed to be itchy. Goodnight, Journal!

March 16th

I found Dad out back when I got home from school. He was crying. When he heard me coming he went inside. But it looked like he was holding one of Mom's dresses in one hand and some weird looking book in the other. And I think his hand was bleeding? I don't know what to do. I wish he would talk to me, like he used to.

In less-weird news, Reed said I make a great angel. I think he's being nice, too. Everyone

is just so nice all the time. Sometimes I can't stand it. I only have one line, I can't be all that good. I know that they feel bad for me. Well, I have a report due so I have to get back to work. Goodnight, Journal!

P.S. My back must be getting two horrible pimples. It's still itchy and there are bumps now. Two of them. Why me??

March 18th

I am going crazy. These bumps are getting bigger. It's so bizarre because they're actually hard, like a bone or something. I asked Madison to touch one and she said it was, "the worst thing that ever happened to her."

They are still itchy, but a little less now. I think I should go to Dad, but it's hard to. The bumps are where my bra straps are and I don't know how to show him without feeling super awkward. I feel like a freak. What should I do? Mom would know how to fix this. Wish she was here. Sometimes I wish I could just trade and have her back, and Dad had been the one in that car. But I know I shouldn't think about things like that. It's really horrible of me.

Goodnight, Journal.

March 20th

Dear Diary,

My Aunt Allie and little cousin Ben came over for lunch today. They brought baked ziti. When I was outside with Ben he said, "My mom told me that your mommy is an angel in Heaven now." I told him that I didn't want to talk about it, and he asked why not. Kids are so stupid.

I asked my aunt to look at my back. She acted kind of grossed out. She told me that it looks like a skin infection. She said that if she didn't know better, she'd think I'm growing feathers. (!!!!) She said she'd talk to my dad about getting me to the dermatologist right away. I have to hide in gym class when I get changed now. I hate it.

Anyway, goodnight Journal.

March 25th

Dear Diary,

I'm starting to freak out. I keep asking my dad when he's going to take me to the doctor. He says, "not long now." When is that exactly? I asked to stay home from school today and Dad said yes. It's the last day before spring break. Maybe I should have gone and shown the nurse again. I'm just really confused.

The bumps are bigger every day. I found a feather on my sheet last night. I don't know what to do. Goodnight Journal.

March 30th

Dear Diary,

Something is up with Dad. I'm really scared. My back feels horrible and he won't talk to me. I went into his room and I found Mom's wedding dress laid out on his bed. He found me and asked what I was doing there. He even had her shoes laid out, and her purse, like he was expecting her to come walking back in.

I called Madison and she doesn't know what to do either. I keep begging him to take me to the doctor. Maybe I should call my aunt. It's late now. I'll call in the morning.

Goodnight Journal.

April 3rd

Dear Diary,

I officially have feathers. I need help so bad. I can't stop crying.

My cell phone has been missing for a few days. I don't know what happened to it. I do think Dad might have taken it. He won't let me go to Reed's house or to play practice. He said that I need to stay home and rest. He stands and blocks the door when I try to leave. I wish I knew what to do. I really miss mom. I would give anything to have her here. Why couldn't it have been the other way around?

Goodnight Journal. Please help.

April 5th

I think I'm going nuts, because last night I heard something. I walked past Dad's room and I heard him praying or something. He kept saying my mom's name like, "Helen, Helen, come back soon, I can't wait any longer, this is too much," and things like that. He said that he was "holding up his end of the deal." What does he mean by that?

And I must be going crazy, because I thought I heard her answer. I know it's not possible. But it was a lot like Mom's voice, but there were also all these other whispers. It was hard to understand her.

I think it sounded like she said, "Soon."

Anyway. Goodnight, Journal. Dad's calling me downstairs for some reason.

THE GATHERING: AN APRIL FOOL'S TALE

Brian studied his calendar. He picked up a thick black marker and crossed out a square. March was over. Tomorrow he would attend the gathering.

His bag was packed and his car was loaded up. He kissed his wife goodbye with the same false cheer that he did every year.

"Have fun, honey!" wished his wife, "Tell the boys that I say hi."

"Will do," Brian promised as he grabbed his keys and headed for the door. He crossed the front yard and climbed into his car. He started the ignition. And then he sighed.

As it often did, Brian's father's voice chimed in his head. *'The only way to do something is to do it.'*

That was usually enough to propel him onto the road toward his destination: Johnston, Iowa, his hometown. Where else would the gathering be held?

...

They always met at the same little pub. Was it called Joe's now? It didn't matter. They arrived separately around 8 pm. From there, the handshake-hugs began, the pats on the backs, the how-ya-beens.

Aaron's son scored a homerun in the last game of the season. Greg's father started dialysis. Jared's wife was now pregnant—with twins, no less. Dean was almost through his residency. And Brian? He was busy remodeling his kitchen.

Rounds of beer were gulped and piles of wings demolished. The other patrons in the bar occasionally glanced their way to see what all the laughter was about.

After the catching up and jokes were out of the way, the group began to wind down. A silence settled over them. They sipped the last of their drinks and waited for someone to speak the words they'd rather not hear.

Brian sucked in a deep breath. "Okay, then. We should go."

A few of his friends nodded. One or two of them stared at the table. Nevertheless, they paid their tab, gathered their jackets, and left the pub.

It was only a short walk to the cemetery. The gathering was about to begin.

…

Brian could have found the grave in his sleep. He walked the path once per year, but he had each step committed to memory. Go straight through the entrance, then left at the elm tree, straight again past the tall steeple-topped memorial stone and right at the broken iron fence. There, not twenty feet ahead, was the grave of Charles Acker.

The group stood quietly in a semi-circle, heads bowed.

"Who wants to start?" asked Jared, pushing up his glasses.

Silence hung in the air.

"I will," said Greg. He cleared his throat. "Hey, Charlie. Happy April first...I can't believe it's been twenty years. But we're all here to see you. We have a lot to tell you this time around." Greg glanced around the group. "Got some good news and some bad news. My dad's health isn't so great these days. You remember my dad, right? He took us fishing out at Lake Red Rock one year."

"That was a great trip, man," chimed Aaron.

Greg nodded. "It was a great trip."

"Hey Brian, isn't that when a bee stung your left buttcheek?"

The group laughed. Brian grinned. "Yeah. It was the best trip ever."

Greg went on, "His kidneys aren't doing so great. But the doctors are hopeful."

"Speaking of doctors," added Brian, "Dean here is almost a full-fledged surgeon. Can you believe that?"

"That and a plague of locusts is how you know the world is about to end," laughed Aaron.

The group chuckled. "When we were kids did you ever think that there would be a time when people would actually *pay* Dean to take a knife to them?"

"I can't believe it now!" quipped Brian.

Another round of laughter.

Jared spoke up, "Chuck, man, I wish you could be here to meet my little girls. They'll be here soon. I'm going to tell them all about their Uncle Charlie, about all the funny things he used to say and do." Jared's head hung forward. "I'm just really sorry that you won't be here to meet them."

A hush fell over the group.

Brian went next. "I'm sorry too, Charlie."

"Yeah, man. It doesn't go away. It's not right, what happened."

More silence.

"We can tell you a million times over that it was an accident. We just meant it to be a joke...like all the other things. It was just all a bunch of stupidity for the sake of a few laughs. We had no idea that limb was going to break. How could we?" asked Brian.

"We were going to come back for you in a few, Chuck. It's not like we planned to leave you up in that tree all night," added Jared.

Dean shuddered. "Sometimes, late at night, right before I'm about to fall asleep, I can still hear that *snap!*"

Greg looked down, face grim. "And you don't mean the sound of the branch, do you?"

The huddled clump of men shared a collective shiver.

"What can we say? We were complete idiots. Now we're here, and you're not. And that's never going to be okay," said Brian.

"Amen," nodded Greg. "Every time I see someone wearing a red cap, I think of him. You know, I swear sometimes I can even smell that Big Red gum he was always chewing."

"I thought I was the only one." replied Dean, "Do you ever hear him smacking away? Like when you're falling asleep?" Dean imitated cow-like chomping.

The group laughed softly, despite their best efforts not to.

"What about that funny whistle-y panting he did when he had to run in gym class?" added Aaron, who then demonstrated a nasal huffing through his nostrils.

"Or the way he'd always want to high five us even when there was nothing high five worthy?" added Jared.

'Hey guys, I read this cool comic! High five!'

'We have pizza for lunch today! High five!'

'My cat, Peanut, took a piss yesterday! High five!'

By now the group was in hysterics.

After some wiping of eyes and clearing of throats, they began to calm down. Brian suddenly felt the urge to avoid all eye contact with his old pals. He stared at his feet.

"...Anyway, we should probably get going."

"Yeah, man," seconded Jared. "Okay, Chuck, we'll see you in a year. Take care of yourself, man."

"Goodbye, Charlie."

"Catch you later, Charlie-boy!"

"Don't be a stranger, now."

"Have some respect, Aaron!" chastised Brian, as he led the pack away from Charlie's final resting place.

...

"Hey Bri, can I catch a ride back with you? I'm still a little buzzed." asked Greg.

"Sure thing man, where are you staying?"

The group chatted as they began their walk to the front of the cemetery.

"At the motel on the east end of town," said Greg. "The Rest Inn."

"Yeah, no problem. I'm staying there too." Brian looked around. "But maybe someone else should drive us both. I'm clearly too drunk to find our way out of here. Didn't we pass this stump before?"

"I thought so too," said Dean.

"Me too," said Aaron. "I feel like we should be at the gate by now."

"Okay, well, this place isn't that big," said Jared. "Does anyone have a flashlight?"

"I do on my phone," said Brian, whipping out his cell. He turned on the flash and shone it over the tombstones. "Where is...where are we?"

"We just got turned around. Look, the exit is this way," Greg took the lead and began to march forward. The rest followed in tow.

Brian almost tripped on something. He looked down and aimed the light on his foot.

He was standing on a red baseball cap.

Brian bent down and picked it up. He held it to the light.

"Okay. Who did this?"

"Did what, man?" Dean winced at the light. "What is it?"

"It's a red cap. Who did this?"

The men's eyes bounced from face to face.

"Why would any of us do that, Brian?"

"As a prank? To be funny? Whoever did this can go to hell."

"Woah, Bri, calm down," Greg approached, hands up in surrender. "None of us did this, man. Relax. Someone probably dropped it."

Brian looked around the group. His shoulders slumped.

"You're right. I'm sorry. I just, I want to get out of here."

"You're not the only one. So let's go." This time it was Aaron who led the charge.

...

"We have been by this same broken fence fifteen times," announced Dean.

"I don't understand. I could find this place in my sleep." Brian had ditched the red cap and was now watching the last percentage of his cell battery drain away. "How could we have gotten lost here?"

31

"Maybe they changed things around since last year?" asked Greg.

Jared's head whipped back. "Yeah Greg, people love it when their dead family members are dug up and moved for no reason."

"Well I'm just saying, I thought I saw an open grave a while back.Maybe they're relocating some people. Maybe there's a problem with the soil or...hell, I don't know. I'm so tired."Greg sighed. "Can we sit a minute? We've been walking for an hour now."

"I could use a rest, too," said Brian.

The group dropped onto the soft, dewy grass.

"Maybe we should call someone."

"Call who? None of us live around here anymore."

"And if they ask why we're here, what do we say? We're visiting our deceased childhood friend at midnight, just because it's fun?"

"No. We don't talk about this," Dean said with finality. "We didn't then. We don't now."

Greg nodded, "Okay, yeah, cool. But we've been walking in circles and we still can't find the damn exit. I don't really feel like sleeping in a cemetery tonight, but if—"

"Hey, shhh, wait," Aaron interjected. "Do you smell that?"

"Smell what?"

"It's...cinnamon."

Brian sniffed the air.

"It's definitely cinnamon..." continued Aaron. "Like... "

"Like chewing gum," said Brian.

The group looked around wildly. They rose to their feet, cell phones flying out of pockets for more light.

"Hello? Who's there? Come out you sick freak."

"We know you're out there. This isn't funny, man, so come on out."

"Come out now and we won't kick your ass!"

They were met with nothing more than a still and silent night. In the distance, an owl hooted.

Brian grabbed Greg's arm. "Let's just go, we gotta go. The exit has to be up ahead."

...

"What time is it?" croaked Jared.

Brian looked down at his phone. "Sorry. Phone's dead.

"It's almost midnight," said Aaron.

Brian's feet were throbbing. His head was beginning to ache. "Did you say it's almost twelve o'clock?"

"Yeah, man."

"Huh," nodded Brian.

"What, Bri?"

"Nothing." Brian willed his legs to keep slogging through the wet grass.

Dean spoke up next, "Guys...what time was it?"

"Was what?"

"When it happened," Dean huffed. "What time did...what time did Charlie fall?"

"Oh." Aaron looked down. "Maybe 11:30, quarter til?"

"It was at 11:53," replied Greg.

An uncomfortable quiet fell over the group.

"Stop. Whatever anyone is thinking, just stop it now," said Jared. When no one responded, he added, "It will be light out soon. We'll be able to see the exit and get the hell out of here. We'll be home before we know it, and we'll never come to this—" Jared grunted as he fell forward.

Brian looked down and reached out a hand to help his friend. "You okay, man? What got you there?"

Jared climbed to his feet. "I don't know, I think...it's that damn, busted fence."

Brian shook his head, "That's not possible. The broken fence isn't far from Chuck's grave. We can't have circled back again."

"Possible or not, Bri, it's happening."

Brian heaved a sigh. He dropped his head back and rubbed his neck. As he stared at the dark sky, he noticed a red ring circling the moon.

"Blood moon..." he whispered. Something suddenly tugged at his attention. It was a noise. It was...chewing.

Chomp, chomp, chomp.

Brian spun around. "Who is *doing* that!" he demanded.

"Doing what?" Aaron blinked at him, startled.

"Doing what? Chewing! Who is chewing gum like that!"

"Brian, man, nobody is..." Aaron tilted his head. "Oh, god. I hear it too."

The group fell stone still. They all listened. *Chomp, chomp, chomp.*

Greg cursed. Dean groaned.

"Shut up! Shh!" Brian raised a hand to silence them.

Not just chewing. There was another noise. Whistling breath.

"We need to get the hell out of here. Now."

Brian took off. He wasn't sure where he was going, just that he needed to get there immediately. His friends lumbered beside him, bumping into his arms and nearly tripping him with their feet.

One of them let out a shout. His voice vanished as Brian heard a *thump!*

Brian spun around. He looked frantically from face to face. He saw Aaron, Jared, Dean and—where was Greg?

"Greg!" He barked. "Greg!"

"I'm down here!"

Greg's voice came from a hole in the ground, some ten feet behind him.

No, not a hole— a grave.

Brian trudged forward. "Greg, let's go," he extended his arm downward as he approached the open plot. His friends tailed behind him, cell phone flashlights swinging as they moved.

For a moment, the light caught on the tombstone. It was shiny. Brand new.

Greg clung to Brian's arm. Brian grunted as he hauled his friend from the earth. With Greg back on solid ground, Brian studied the grave again.

"Someone, shine a light here."

Dean held his phone up and pointed it at the stone. Brian read aloud. "Here lies Greg Smith, Sept. 1 1984-April 1st, 2019."

Brian paused. He then turned toward Greg.

"What the hell, man?" Greg backed away slowly. "What the hell? If this is one of you..."

"It wasn't one of us, Greg." Brian grabbed Dean's arm and directed his flashlight down the row of headstones. "Look."

Five open graves. Five shiny, new headstones.

And one small, whistling silhouette standing in the distance.

THE LETTER: A MOTHER'S DAY TALE

March 9th, 1983

Dear Anna and Lee,

How's the weather in the motherland? We've had a lot of rain here so I can't imagine what it's like in London right now!

Well, Drakie is turning seven this year and starting to get a better concept of holidays. It's fun to watch your children change over the years. It wasn't long ago he was screaming on Santa's lap, arms stretched out for me. Now he makes us Christmas cards, Valentine's hearts, and glittery paper Easter Eggs. The problem is that he is overly aware of where these treasures end up at times. The next phase of understanding will hopefully include a concept of fridge surface area and the spatial limitations it presents.

Drake has been getting better at drawing lately—growing by leaps and bounds, I would say. Every parent thinks their child is special and I guess I'm no exception! It seems every day he surprises me. He's been excelling in math, to the point that his teachers want to bump him up a grade or two. He's also a wonder with languages. I caught him watching the Spanish channel the other night. I asked him what he was doing, and he said, *"Que, mamasita?"* But here's the amazing thing about it—it's like he wasn't even aware that he wasn't speaking English!

I wish I could take all the credit. John and I have worked very hard at raising him to be a good and happy boy. But the truth is that I think he has some stellar genes. One day we'll have to explain about the adoption, but I just don't think he's ready yet.

There's no such thing as a perfect child, and Drakie has his challenges. He struggles to make friends sometimes. It hurts to see him try to fit in and be met with rejection so often. I suspect he feels lonely. But good news, his teacher is a kind woman and has set him up with a pen pal! Drake was so excited to write his first letter and insisted he do it on his own. He can be independent—stubborn even, and that he definitely gets from me. I'm sure you're well aware of this, Anna! Haha!

How are the girls? Are they looking forward to Easter? What's Easter like there, anyway?

Lots of love to you and yours,

Cindy

...

March 30th, 1983

Dear Lee and Anna,

Those pictures you sent were so cute! I love the girls' Easter bonnets. Who knew that they still made those? What a laugh! I can't wait to visit you. Loralei is getting so tall! She really looks just like Lee. (Sorry, Anna! That's just how it goes!) Anna, I'm so glad to hear about your promotion. Does that mean more hours in the field?

We're good here. John's been busy with work. What else is new, right? I joined a book club, but I doubt I'll have time to attend very often. Between work and being a mom, it's all I can do to get a few hours of sleep at night!

Drakie has been over the moon about writing letters to his pen pal. He reads them right away and starts to work on his response immediately after. I helped him write his letter—or I tried anyway. He wants to do it on his own, and I could tell he wanted to get it just right. It's amazing how quickly he learned to write in full, complex sentences. His handwriting is really good, too! I think it's a bit better than mine!

Dad is doing well. We had him over for dinner last night. He is getting so gray all of the sudden. He asked you to call him if you all have time! Well, we're off to a movie!

Lots of love to you all,

Cindy

...

April 13th, 1983

Dear Lee and Anna,

Dad was so happy you called! I haven't seen him smile like that in a while. It was sweet. He thinks you're starting to pick up an English accent. At least some of us in this family will finally have some class, haha! We all sure do miss you here. We're doing okay enough, I guess, but it will be so nice to see your faces again.

Drake's teacher called home yesterday. She said that Drake has been upsetting some of the other children. The kids said that he was talking "backwards" while in the bathroom stall. I'm not sure what that means. When I ask him about, Drake just shrugs. He's been a little quiet lately. Whatever happened, it was enough to bother his friends. I wish I understood him a little better sometimes.

Anna, you were a strange kid too. I know I wasn't—haha! And since this is a letter you can't argue with me about it. Have you all experienced something like this? What do you do when the girls have a hard time with friends?

How's the new title, Anna? Are they working you to the bone? Sure hope not!

Well, I gotta go. The mail's here and Drakie just has to read his letter. He's so secretive about these things! He guards them with his life! It's got me so curious.

Hugs and kisses to all,

Cindy

. . .

April 25th, 1983

Dear Anna and Lee,

I'm a little rattled. Drake's behavior at school is getting worse. Apparently there was an incident where he stood up in the middle of class, pointed at a little girl, and made a very strange sound. His teacher said that it sounded like "TV static." She said she couldn't explain it any better. She seemed pretty rattled by this.

I notice he's becoming very possessive about his letters. He snatches them away the moment I take them from the mailbox. He asks to check the mail no less than three times a day. Even on Sunday. I asked to see the letters and he just stared at me for a while and then said, very calmly, "No. They're for me, and not you."

I'm going to try to get a look at them while he's asleep tonight. He keeps them in a box under his bed. Is that a breach of trust and privacy? What do you think?

Anna, so glad to hear you're enjoying your new position. And Amanda winning the spelling bee—wow, big news! Congratulations, sweetie! You must have studied so hard!

Wishing you all well,

Cindy

...

May 7th, 1983

Dear Anna,

I don't know if you'd mind keeping this from Lee. I'm not sure how to handle this. I read through Drake's letters. They started out normal enough, talking about favorite toys and asking what he likes to do for fun, and so on. I thought that they might have been written by a little girl. But something started to feel off about them a few letters in. They began to tell him what a great child he is and how he is "living up to his fullest potential."

I'm not sure who is writing to my son, but they sign their letters, "Mother."

I called his teacher right away and asked how she assigned this pen pal. And Anna, she actually said to me, "What pen pal?" She knew nothing about this. And I'm not sure how to handle the situation. I would have called you, but Drake seems to always be listening in lately. He is perpetually hovering in a doorway, never out of earshot. I know that if I try to take these letters from him, he's going to have a fit.

We address the letters to someone in Chile. I tried looking up the name, but I doubt that it's a real name, anyway. I'm going to reach out to the social worker who helped us with the adoption. Maybe they can help shed some light on this.

I'm sorry, how are Lee and the girls? Miss you all. Oh, and Happy Mother's Day!

Love you kiddo,

Cindy

...

May 18th, 1983

Anna,

Thanks for the call the other day. I'm glad you were able to sneak that in while you were at work. Sorry for whispering, I was at my desk. It helped so much to hear your voice!

I was able to get ahold of Donna from the adoption agency. She didn't have any new information for me. As we already know, Drake was a hospital drop off. There is no way to determine the identities of his birth parents. And she said that of course they wouldn't give away our home address, even if the biological parents did request it.

Drake asked why I didn't hang his Mother's Day card on the fridge. I didn't have the heart to tell him that there is something different and a little upsetting about it. His handwriting looks so...odd. It's like he wrote it with his left hand. I asked his teacher if she noticed something strange about his writing lately, and she agreed that it wasn't up to his usual standard.

John and I have scheduled to take Drake to the doctor. We don't even know what to tell him is wrong. We just know that something isn't right.

I tried to find the letters again, but Drake moved the box. Tonight at dinner, he asked if I'd been in his room when he was at school. He stared at me and I felt like he knew I had been looking. But how could he? He is always so serious lately. I never see him play anymore.

I miss my little boy.

Hope your girls are well,

Cindy

...

May 31st, 1983

Anna,

I did what you suggested, and I took the newest letter straight from the mailbox and hid it from him. He asked me many times about the mail and it was difficult to keep the truth from him. He just seems to look at me and know what I'm thinking. It's a little frightening at times.

But here's what's really bothering me. The letter I opened made absolutely no sense. It wasn't written in English or any other language I could identify. The letters, if I can call them that, were like little boxes. I showed it to John and he has no idea what it is. He thinks we should take this to the police. I think he might be right.

As I tucked Drake into bed last night, I kissed him and told him that I loved him so much. As I went to leave his room, he said, "You've always done well for me, Mom." What child says these things?

The doctor wasn't able to find any explanation, either. Everything looked perfectly normal. I guess there's one issue—they weren't able to determine his blood type. But that could simply be a problem with the test.

Please keep in touch,

Cindy

...

June 10th, 1983

Anna,

Don't show this to Lee or the girls.

Please tell me one thing. Tell me that you remember my little boy. Drake's been gone for three days. I am hysterical. But nobody seems to remember that he exists. What is going on here? I would have called, but John keeps watching me. He acts like I'm crazy. I don't trust him. You're all I have left.

The last time I saw Drakie, he was standing at the end of our bedroom. A light was shining in from the windows and it woke me up. It was the middle of the night. Our clock even stopped at the exact time—3:21 a.m.

He stood there in his little pajamas, but it seemed like he wasn't alone. I can't explain it. I saw some sort of figures out of the corner of my eye. They were slender, maybe white or gray. I wanted to get up and go to him, but I felt like I couldn't. I felt weighed down, glued to the bed. And when he spoke, I don't think I saw his lips move.

He said, "Thank you, Mommy," and then he was gone. All of it was gone—the light, the figures, and my son.

Anna, please help me. You have to help me find my boy. Dad doesn't remember him. And Drake's photos, his artwork, they're all missing. I went to the police and they say that there is no record of Drake, not in the township, not at school, nothing. But I know I have a son, and he'll always be mine. Please, Anna, I know that I'm his mother.

Please say you know it, too.

Cindy

THE EXHIBIT: AN INDEPENDENCE DAY TALE

Mark had worked at the American History Museum for two and a half years. In that time, he had done his fair share of grunt work, from moving the entire contents of the archive to its new home in the basement level to repairing the flooded, second-story women's restroom. He'd even filled in as the emergency IT person in a pinch. There were two things that got him out of bed in the morning: his love of history and the joy he felt seeing the smiles on children's faces as they toured these beloved, if humble, halls.

Lately, Mark had been handed some fun assignments, and this was no exception. He was to arrange the diorama to depict a scene of the signing of the Declaration of Independence, to be debuted on the Fourth of July. Mark had scoured the storage room for the appropriate backdrop mural. When he could not locate one, he put in a request to commission a new canvas—and to his surprise, it was granted. This, more than anything else, told Mark that he was moving up the ranks from a 'no one' to a 'someone.'

Mark had invited his family to see the modest opening of this historical diorama. So excited was his mother that she wrangled in whatever relatives were willing to skip their backyard barbecues in favor of viewing his display in person. It was a fair bit of pressure, and Mark was determined to get it right.

Despite much careful planning, Mark found himself toiling into the night in the week leading up to Independence Day. The mannequins he ordered had arrived late, their costumes ill-fitting and in need of resewing. Mark repurposed old props, dummies, and furniture where and when possible. He had assembled just enough material to complete the project, but he was running out of time.

It was 10:03 p.m. and Mark found himself adjusting John Hancock's wig for the third time. No matter what he did, it never seemed to sit properly. The museum was empty, save for Mark and his painted, plastic friends.

"And let's move you over here, Bennie," Mark dragged a portly body across the carpet. He propped it against the wall. "Wish you'd learn to stand up on your own." He sighed and rubbed his eyes. Mark reassessed the scene again. He wanted to feature this particular founding father more prominently, but the figure was not weighted properly and was prone to tipping over. "Not a good look for Big Ben Franklin, is it?"

Mark nearly leapt from his skin when a voice responded.

"No, it's not."

Mark lost his grip on the dummy and it crashed to the floor. Mark spun around. "Who's there?"

"Didn't mean to scare you, my friend," the janitor offered him an apologetic smile.

"Oh, it's you, Tom," Mark laughed in relief.

"The one and only," the janitor nodded. He had a kind face, with crinkles around his eyes and a perpetual five o'clock shadow. "I'm sorry I startled you."

Mark straightened up. "It's nothing. No need to apologize!"

Tom leaned on his mop. He looked down at the body of Ben Franklin. "Maybe I'm apologizing to the wrong one. I've always been fond of Big Ben."

"Ah, yeah, me too." Mark knelt down and hoisted the figure up. "I think he'll pull through. He survived gout, didn't he?"

"Guess he did." Tom chuckled. He observed the diorama from afar. "Not too shabby, Mark."

"Yeah? You think so?" Mark steadied the dummy against the wall again, willing it to stay put.

"It's really coming together," praised Tom. "Say, what are you planning to do with that one left out in storage?"

Mark was occupying himself with examining Ben's face. The mannequin had sustained a scratch on its cheek during its fall. He sighed. "Sorry, Tom, the what?"

"Well, I noticed another one of your friends here down in the artifacts room. Wasn't with the other guys anymore. Figured you took it out. Want me to bring it up for you?"

Mark stopped fussing with Ben's lacy collar and looked up. "You say there's a mannequin in artifacts storage? You're sure?"

Tom scratched his beard. "Well, I'm no expert, but I think I know a dummy when I see one."

"Huh." Mark ran a hand through his hair. "I don't remember taking any moreof them out. But no one else has a key to the mannequin locker right now...so it must have been me. Wonder who I'm missing?" Mark studied the scene, ticking off key founding fathers in his head.

"Couldn't tell you," replied Tom.

"Well, what did it look like?" Mark asked.

"Hard to say," the janitor answered, "It was covered up with a sheet. Well, I'll be heading home now. Don't work too hard."

Mark stared after the janitor's retreating form. "Oh… yeah. Hey, thanks. Have a good night."

…

"I knew he was messing with me."

Mark had descended the two flights of stairs to grab paint with the hope of fixing poor Ben's cheek. He passed through artifacts storage on his way out to determine which of his mannequins was on the lam. He found the room to be devoid of plastic bodies, covered in sheets or otherwise.

Mark began to climb the stairs. It was getting late. He checked his watch and sighed. 3:02 in the morning. Mark was ready to groan, but a different noise sounded first.

It was a soft *clink, clink, clink,* and just barely audible. It sounded like something dragging across the linoleum, heavy and rattling. It came from above, perhaps around the top landing of the staircase.

Mark paused. He leaned over and peeked up the stairwell.

"Hello?" He called. "Is anyone there?"

The sound stopped.

Mark continued to climb the stairs, more cautiously this time. If anyone were to open the door and leave the staircase, he would hear it. He readied his hand on his cell phone as he reached the landing.

There's nothing here, you idiot, thought Mark as he inspected the empty space.

"It's late," he told himself, "You're just tired.. No worries."

He only needed to adjust a few details, and then he could go home and get some sleep. But first, coffee.

…

Ben had pulled through surgery just fine. His cheek didn't look quite as good as new, but it would be acceptable from a short distance. What's more, somehow, Mark had gotten the dummy to stand independently.

Mark had guzzled not one, but two cups of instant coffee. It tasted bitter and artificial, but it gave him the boost he needed to finish the project.

With most of the major elements of the scene finished, Mark was engrossed in adjusting the mannequin of Thomas Jefferson. He had decided to sit Jefferson at the desk, his arm poised over the Declaration of Independence, to depict the act of the signing taking place.

Easier said than done, it turned out. The statues were rigid and their joints stiff. It was difficult to achieve the natural look he was after.

Mark's concentration was broken when he heard a crash just behind him.

Mark's head snapped up. He quickly scanned the area. Nothing moved. Then, slowly, a paint can rolled into view, dripping red liquid onto the floor.

Mark froze. He had used that very can of paint to finish the faux walls of the diorama. It couldn't have fallen on its own. Mark was not alone.

A brief search produced only one suitable weapon. Quietly as he could, Mark picked up a hammer and began to creep toward the red trail that stretched in front of him.

Mark turned the corner of the diorama. He readied himself for action.

He wasn't sure if he was relieved or angry when he found nothing more than a puddle of red paint. It must have fallen from the workbench he'd carelessly set it on.

Mark turned to look for a towel when something tugged at the corner of his eye.

Standing between Mark and the diorama was a mannequin. At least, he assumed it must be. It was impossible to tell, as it was—as Tom had described—draped in a sheet.

The paint had splattered in every direction, including onto the white cotton covering this plastic figure. Speckled in red blotches and motionless under the fabric, the mannequin appeared every inch a sinister spirit slipped from beyond the veil.

But wait, get a grip, Mark argued with himself. *Of course this isn't a mannequin.*

The alternative was hardly less comforting. Why would someone do this to him? Did they want his exhibit to be a failure?

Mark clenched the hammer tighter in one fist. "All right, then. Okay. You have my attention." Mark took one small step forward. "I just need to know, who are you?"

The paint-splattered wraith did not respond. It simply stood in an inhuman way.

Mark took another step forward. "I don't want any trouble. I won't report you. Whatever you're doing, it's not too late to just leave."

Nothing. Not a word emitted from the figure. Not a sound.

Mark continued his slow approach. "Tom, if this is you, you've had your laugh. This was a great gag. Very clever, good setup. Maybe this is a hazing or a pre-opening night tradition. I get it, I do. But I need to get back to work now."

Still nothing.

Mark stopped several feet away from the shrouded figure.

He raised his arm, reaching gingerly for the sheet.

No sooner had his fingertips touched the unnaturally hard shoulder beneath the cotton, the being began to move.

Mark cursed as he scrambled backward, desperate to distance himself from this entity.

The crimson-stained fabric dragged across the floor as the specter lurched forward. Its steps were short, stunted, and gave its gait a jerking quality. Mark recognized the *clink, clink, clink* sound from the stairwell earlier that night.

Mark almost tripped over the renegade paint can. "W-w-wait—" he exhaled, still shuffling backwards. "Please, whatever you want, you can have it."

The being stalked forward, unrelenting. Mark brandished the hammer in front of him,

"Take another step closer and I'll use this," he threatened. Mark winced when he heard the quiver in his voice.

On it marched, undeterred. Mark backed away until he was a few short paces from the entrance to the stairwell.

He made a run for it. Mark barreled into the landing. He checked briefly for a lock on the door, but there was none. Without further delay, Mark leapt down the stairs, two or three at a time.

When he reached the bottom of the staircase, he stopped to listen.

Clink, clink, clink.

The sound echoed from the top of the landing. It was following him.

Mark ran into the archive room. He closed the door behind him. With shaking hands, he pulled out his key ring and began to fumble through them, searching feverishly for the correct key.

This was taking too long. He would try again in the next room and get more of a lead on the entity. Mark jammed the keyring into his pocket and passed through to the artifacts storage room.

Once again he clicked the door shut and reached for his keys. *Except, they weren't there.* With a sinking feeling, he realized that he must have missed his pocket and dropped them on the floor. Mark stilled and held his breath. He was sure that, very faintly, he could clear the metallic rattle of the being as it drew near. There would be no going back for the keys.

Mark patted his pants, searching for his phone. He cursed himself for leaving it upstairs.

Think, think dammit!

With a prolonged creak, he heard the door to the archives room open. After a moment, the shuttering steps of the creature began anew.

Mark looked for anything with which he could block the door. The best he could find was a stack of boxes. He shoved the tower towards the door, then leaned against it, panting.

Mark circled the room like a caged animal. He examined the half window. No luck there; it had no latch and was too small to squeeze through, even if he busted the glass. He looked for more objects to push against the door.

Too late. The clinking grew louder, closer, and then it stopped. Mark watched the door, his heart in his throat. The handle turned, and with an unpleasant *scraaape*, the boxes began to slide forward.

Mark was left with one option: to keep going. Unfortunately, there was only one room left. Mark took a breath and exited the room. He headed for the general storage area, which was, regrettably, also home to the mannequin locker.

This area of the museum always reminded Mark of a basement or a parking garage. Bulky items, such as plastic trees, old banners and retired preserved animals lined the walls. It was never a pleasant place to visit at night, due to the lack of natural light and the beady eyes that seemed to track every step he took. But it had at least two saving graces: one was the overhead flood lights, the other was the walk up to the cellar doors. If Mark could make it through to the other side—and why wouldn't he?—he would be out and into the rear alley in no time.

Mark slid his hand along the wall and flipped on the lights.

He doubled back, blinking rapidly in the light. There were dozens of them—no, there must have been fifty or more! Every direction he looked, there they stood.

Gone were the mountain lions, frozen eternally in mid-snarl. Gone were the stacks of pallets and the plastic trees. Stretched between Mark and the cellar doors were row after row of sheet-covered mannequins.

Mark's stomach turned. He sagged against the wall. *What was this?* He hoped to wake up in his warm bed, relieved to know that this was all a nightmare. It wasn't, however, and there would be only one way out.

Mark took one trembling step forward. They remained still. He lifted his foot, softly, gently, and took another. The bodies were motionless.

As Mark weaved through them, he observed that they were of all shapes and sizes. Some towered over him, some had sloped shoulders, some appeared hunched, and some were very petite and child-like in stature. The problem was, in all of Mark's time spent at the museum, he had never seen a single juvenile mannequin.

He tried to shove these thoughts from his mind. Only one thing mattered, and that was getting out of here.

On and on they went. Mark was vigilant not to inadvertently touch the figures, which required some careful ducking and contorting on his part. The cellar walk-up was in sight now, the glowing EXIT sign humming above the steel doors.

There was one cloaked being that particularly drew Mark's eye. It was the smallest in the room, and it lay between Mark and the exit. It didn't stand like the others, but instead it rested on the floor, wrapped in the sheet to form an oval shaped bundle. Mark stared at it. He thought he discerned the vague outline of a tiny hand shoved against the fabric.

He couldn't step over it and ducking around it would cause him to knock into the other beings. With as much tenderness as he could muster, he reached down and scooped up the tiny mannequin.

No sooner did he touch the swaddled figure, did the beings spring to life.

Mark's heart hammered in his chest as the wraiths turned to look at him with their blind, blank faces. Their sheets swirled across the floor as they began to lurch forward en masse.

"No, please—" Mark squeezed the bundle to his chest. He backed toward the steel doors, searching for the handle with one hand.

The nearest being stepped closer to him. It was shorter, with rounded shoulders, and it appeared to look up into his eyes. Beneath the sheet he could just make out the curve of a cheekbone, the gentle slope of a nose.

In his panic, Mark had failed to notice that the tiny, hard figure in his arms began to move as well. It…it was reaching for something. It was reaching for the being in front of him.

Mark shook. "Oh…" he stammered. "Oh…"

Cradling the small bundle in both hands, he reached out and offered it to the specter.

To his surprise, the being accepted it very gently into its arms. It tucked the bundle against its breast. And then it nodded.

…

It was in this way that Nancy Hoffman, director of the American History Museum, received Mark Snyder's resignation on her desk the following morning.

In it, Mark thanked her for his time in her employ. His explanation for leaving the position was sparse at best, and perplexing. He simply stated, "I'm ready to really learn now."

Mark had left behind a complete and portrait-accurate depiction of the signing of the declaration. Only one thing was odd: the mannequin's quill tips were all dripping with red paint.

THE CLIENT: A HALLOWEEN STORY

Service date: 9/12/2018

Client name: Ramsay, Ellen

Diagnosis: F21.5 Schizoaffective D/O

Location: Client's Home

Time: 1:45 pm

Assessment: Client was calm, lucid, and friendly. She appeared clean and well groomed. Client denied hearing voices or seeing visions at this time.

SI/HI suspected: No homicidal or suicidal ideation reported.

Service provided: On 9/12/2020, case manager Justin Effort visited Ellen in her home. Client greeted Justin at the door. As this is the first case management home visit, Ellen gave him a tour of the property. Client's home appeared clean, well kept. Client introduced case manager to her "baby," a black cat named Scratch. Client expressed an enjoyment of the season.She indicated that her part-time job at a local tourist museum is going well. She offered case manager a cup of tea, who accepted to build rapport.Client stated she has been tending to her garden. She did not identify any needs at this time.

Staff will follow up on: case manager to continue to monitor for mood and wellness, med compliance.

Service date: 9/27/2018

Client name: Ramsay, Ellen

Diagnosis: F21.5 Schizoaffective D/O

Location: Client's Home

Time: 2:30 pm

Assessment: Client appeared calm, lucid, well rested. Displayed moments of slight mania and/or excitability.

SI/HI suspected: Not at this time.

Service provided: On 9/27/2020, case manager Justin Effort visited Ellen in her home. Client asked to show him her book collection. These books did not appear to be written in English. When asked if client spoke a second language, she responded, "I speak one human tongue." Case manager asked details on this, but client did not respond. Client again offered tea and cookies. Case manager accepted to build rapport. Client continues to work 1-2 days per week. She indicates that she is compliant with all medications. Case manager offered to help client turn in pay stubs to county assistance office to maintain benefits. Client declined.

Staff will follow up on: Continue to monitor for mood, wellness, delusional thinking.

Service date: 10/1/2018

Client name: Ramsay, Ellen

Diagnosis: F21.5 Schizoaffective D/O

Location: Client's Home

Time: 11:00 am

Assessment: Client appeared bright, alert, somewhat nervous. Client was well and formally dressed.

SI/HI suspected: Client denied SI/HI.

Service provided: On 10/1/2018, case manager Justin Effort arrived at client's home. Client did not answer the door. Case manager called client. Client answered the call and indicated she had forgotten about the appointment. Client let case manager into her home. Client offered tea. Case manager accepted to build rapport. Client appeared to have red stain at the bottom of her skirt. When asked about this, she told him that she had been painting her shed outside. Case manager inquired about medication compliance. Client showed him her pill packer. All medications seem to be taken according to specifications. Ellen states she is not hearing voices nor seeing visual hallucinations at this time. Upon leaving the home, case manager observed white feathers stuck to the door frame. Client declined to comment on this.

Staff will follow up on: Case manager to monitor for wellness.

Service date: 10/13/2018

Client name: Ramsay, Ellen

Diagnosis: F21.5 Schizoaffective D/O

Location: Community

Time: 6:00 pm

Assessment: Client was quiet and calm in demeanor.

SI/HI suspected: Denied at this time.

Service provided: On 10/13/2020, case manager Justin Effort saw client at Mack Park. This meeting was unplanned. Client appeared to be watching children play. When approached, client greeted him. Client asked case manager what he was doing at the park. Client then asked if he had any children. CM declined to answer. Case manager asked client if she wanted children. Client answered, "I've been considering them," and laughed. Client stated that work is going well. She indicates that the gift shop has been busy with "tourists and lookie-loo-ers who want a cheap thrill and a cauldron shaped candle."Client then pointed to a child and asked, "Is she yours?" Case manager declined to answer and ended the meeting after confirming next appointment date and time.

Staff will follow up on: Staff to monitor for delusional thinking, paranoia.

Service date: 10/18/2018

Client name: Ramsay, Ellen

Diagnosis: F21.5 Schizoaffective D/O

Location: Community phone call.

Time: 10:10 am.

Assessment: N/A Client not present for call.

SI/HI suspected: N/A

Service provided: On 10/18/2020, case manager Justin Effort received a phone call from Ellen's employer. They indicated that Ellen has not been to work in several days. They also noted that several items are missing from the Trial Exhibit. Case manager attempted to place a phone call to client, but client did not answer. Case manager left a voicemail.

Staff will follow up on: Staff to continue to reach out to client and to reach out to emergency contact if necessary.

Service date: 10/24/2018

Client name: Ramsay, Ellen

Diagnosis: F21.5 Schizoaffective D/O

Location: Community phone call.

Time: 10:01 pm

Assessment: Client sounded calm, quiet. Phone connection was not clear.

SI/HI suspected: N/A

Service provided: On 10/24/2018, case manager Justin Effort received a phone call from Ellen while in the community. He asked client how she has been doing. Client replied she'd been "splendid." Case manager asked about client's job. She stated, "That's all cleared up now." Client said she's been busy preparing for the coming holiday. Case manager observed a high-pitched laughter in the background and asked what the sound was. Client stated she was watching TV. Case manager pointed out that the client does not have a television, per his observation of her home. Client stated that she "meant to say that she was listening to the radio." She apologized for not getting back to him. She said she looked forward to their next appointment.

Staff will follow up on: Case manager to check on client for mood, wellness, med compliance.

Service date: 10/31/2018

Client name: Ramsay, Ellen

Diagnosis: F21.5 Schizoaffective D/O

Location: Client's Home

Time: 12:00 pm

Assessment: Client was calm and quiet. She smiled often. She was formally attired in a long white dress.

SI/HI suspected: Possible homicidal ideation suspected, but not confirmed by client.

Service provided: On 10/31/2020, case manager Justin Effort arrived at client's home. He smelled smoke from the back yard. Case manager went to the backyard to find client standing in front of a large triangle made of sticks, spread across the ground. In the center appeared to be a recently extinguished fire. He asked what client had been doing. Client only said "cooking." Client offered case manager a cup of tea. He declined and left shortly after this. Case manager viewed what appeared to be animal tracks, or hoof prints, on the grass. Case manager to recommend examination by a medical professional, and to reach out to psychiatrist Dr. Wh

Staff will follow up on:

New message received (5:30 pm):

Re: Progress notes

Justin,

Just checking in. As a reminder all notes were due by 5:00 pm today. If you're running behind, please let me know when you expect to finish.

Happy Halloween!

Jana

Service date: 10/31/2018

Client name: Sister Star

Diagnosis: Luminous Transcendence

Location: Case Manager's Home

Time: 11:59 pm

Assessment: The new dawn approaches, and I am filled with the Mother's love.

SI/HI suspected: All life is born from pain. Rebirth is a necessary step toward freedom.

Service provided: Mother thanks you for your gift, friend Justin Effort. The earth is longing to be made whole. A purest child you have offered me. Her sacrifice will not be forgotten. She goes with me willingly now, for she holds truth in her heart and mortal vessel.

Staff will follow up on: She will be honored forevermore. She will be honored forevermore. She will be honored forevermore.

THE HOME: A THANKSGIVING TALE

Amy purchased the home as a foreclosure. Based on the property disclosure, she was not the first to snap up the home at a bargain price. The house boasted such fine bones that she could easily overlook the outdated finishes. Amy assumed that the sizable list of previous owners had tried, and failed, to realize its full potential. But Amy was confident that she could succeed where others had not. She was less sure, however, that she could transform her home in time to host her family's Thanksgiving dinner.

There was no shortage of work to do. Not that she was complaining—she finally had a house of her own. Amy was only too ready to bid farewell to her days of rental payments and lazy landlords.

She was much less prepared, however, for what she found in the wall.

It was just a speck of white paper, jammed none too carefully behind a length of knotty pine paneling. Amy had been a few days into the renovation when the slip fluttered toward the floor like a dusty butterfly. Amy had almost vacuumed it up. In retrospect, she wished she had.

Instead, she read it aloud.

"Hello there," Amy said as she unfolded the paper. "What do we have here?" Amy hoped for a silly greeting, perhaps left by the former owners.

The paper contained three words only. They were written in thin, looping cursive.

"I'm so sorry."

Amy flipped the paper over. Nothing more was written. She flipped it back.

"You're so sorry? What for?"

Amy almost laughed, but felt a sudden unease. She didn't care for this note. Who would have written this? And more importantly, what did they do that was so awful as to warrant a creepy wall message? She struggled between throwing it away and shoving it back into the wall.Finally, into the trash it went. And on with the demolition went Amy.

...

The next few days passed uneventfully. Aside from a wicked splinter in her toe and a staggering home improvement store bill, Amy continued her march towards home makeover bliss.

That was, until she saw it.

The second note was not written on paper, but on the back of a photograph. A polaroid, to be specific. She found the photo resting above a panel of her drop ceiling—soon to be a drywall ceiling, if all went according to plan.

On the back of the photo, in the same thin, looping hand was written,

"I'm so very sorry."

Amy flipped the photo over. It was dim, the details difficult to make out. Where was it taken? Amy could make out a bed in a dark room. A figure appeared to be sleeping on the bed.

It was...a woman? A man? Too dark to tell. Whoever it was, they were wrapped in a blanket and facing away from the camera. What bothered Amy was that the comforter in the photo appeared the same dark navy as her own. It was an uncomfortable coincidence, to be sure.

Amy stared at the picture for a long moment. She wasn't sure what to do. Was this some form of demented diary that the former occupant kept? Unnerved, Amy stuck the photo in her desk drawer.

Amy called her mother that night. She drank a glass of wine. She tried to forget about the strange photograph. After all, no one had been in her home—of course they hadn't. And the holidays were around the corner. All would seem well when surrounded by friends and family.

...

Thanksgiving was a week away. Amy had painted her new walls a soft sage green, her ceilings were now beautifully smooth with crisp white edges. She had planned a menu of all the traditional family favorites, as well as her own personal holiday highlight: caramel pecan pie.

So much to do, so little time, and thankfully no more of it had been wasted looking at spooky photos or secret messages.

Until it was.

This time it was in the bedroom. Amy had despised the old, stained carpet that stretched from wall to wall. She was several feet into pulling it up when she found it. This time, it was not a note or a photograph, but a petite booklet tucked under the carpet padding.

Whoever made this was clearly an artist. Amy flipped through page after page of line drawings, each one etched in thin, delicate curves. She recognized the subject of the sketches: this was her house.

There was something odd about these sketches though. If this book were hidden before she purchased the home, she would expect them to feature wood paneled walls, drop ceilings or even older iterations of the home.

Only the house in these sketches bore an uncanny resemblance to her current home. For Amy, it was too much of a resemblance.

Amy's heart began to race. She turned each page and realized it was a pictorial tour of the property. It started from the outside grounds. Amy recognized the bleeding hearts she planted by the porch, the new black mailbox she placed at the curb.

The guided tour worked its way through the kitchen, where her dining room table stood and her pendant lights gleamed. Then it went through the living room, and up the stairs.

She paused her flipping at the drawing of the second-floor hallway. It was the very same hallway that led to the very same bedroom—the one she was in at that precise moment. She could even see into the master from this angle. And...someone was in there. They were crouched over a book, with their back to the doorway.

No, not someone. Her. It was Amy.

Amy shook her head and muttered, "No, no." Tears burned her eyes. She tossed down the book and made ready to spring to her feet.

The voice was soft and raspy in the doorway behind her.

"I'm so, so very sorry. Welcome home, Amy."

THE WISH: A CHRISTMAS TALE

Theresa clutched her mug, knuckles white as the snow slowly cascading behind two panes of frozen glass. Her face held the same tight, drawn expression that seemed to beset it every December. She reached up and tucked a strand of ash blonde hair behind one ear before sipping gingerly at her coffee.

"Mom?"

"Mm-hm?" The light was winter-pale as it highlighted the thin, shallow lines that began to form at the corners of her face.

"Mom?"

Theresa jumped when a hand slashed through her view of the street. Her eyes darted toward her daughter whose small body conveyed as much pre-teen annoyances it could muster. "Did you hear me?"

Theresa blinked. "Of course." She glanced outside once more. "What time is Kayla coming over?"

Her daughter's exasperated expression reminded Theresa almost comically of herself.

"She's not! I knew you weren't listening. I just told you that she called and asked if I could go over to her house tonight." The young voice teetered with uncertainty in the final moments of her request. She added hastily, "Her dad's car is having problems."

Two blonde eyebrows shot toward the ceiling. "Tonight, Amber?"

"Yeah…" A pause, and then, the challenge, "Why not?"

"Well, for starters," Theresa's coffee swayed in her mug as she swept one arm toward the window, "I don't know if you noticed, but…"

Amber's gaze was sharp as it took in the wintry scene, her voice accusatory. "That's not it, though. Is it?"

At this, Theresa's body tightened. "It's…" She shook her head. "It's not anything. It's Christmas Eve. People usually spend it with their families."

"Most people also look at lights or go shopping at the last minute, too. But not us. We're prisoners every December. We don't even go to visit Grandma or anything." Amber began to comb her fingers through her long, highlighted ponytail. She pulled at the ends. "You know Kayla is moving at the end of the school year. And it's not like it's just anyone, she's my best friend. She wants to bake cookies." And then the clincher. "Her family has presents for me!"

Theresa began to smooth her fingers down her temples. She closed her eyes. "Can you... can you wait for your dad to get home?"

"Dad won't be home until late. He texted." Amber tossed her phone into her mother's lap as evidence. "At least he's allowed to leave the house."

Theresa looked down. So he was. The life of a baker honors no holidays.

Amber seized this moment of quiet to strike. "Please? Please, Mom?" She clasped her hands together and puffed out her lower lip. "It's not even that far! We'll be done in a few hours! I'll be back in time for Charlie Brown." And then, the final blow. The sadness in Amber's voice was earnest and rare. "It's our last Christmas together before she goes."

Theresa groaned. With one final, nervous glance out the window, she reluctantly stood. "Get your coat."

The squeal of glee that escaped her daughter's lips was one she hadn't heard in quite some time. As Theresa gathered her coat, she stared somberly at the fresh, pristine Christmas tree sparkling in the corner of the room. She would remember its warm glow; take with her Bing's soothing tones as she braced herself for the horror to come.

...

When had Theresa first seen her? She could hardly recall. Perhaps she had always been there, watching her from a distance. The thought made Theresa feel ill.

Clouded as childhood memories are, one was preserved with terrible clarity.

Santa's Station. A red, velvety rope. Theresa liked the feel of it under her chubby fingers—like a furry snake. She inched up in line, too small to see the white tufts of Santa's sparkling, snow-covered roof. She was next in line and her mind buzzed with wants and wishes.

The fingers that suddenly curled around her shoulder were as cold as they were unexpected. Theresa turned around, aware only that the icy grasp was very unlike her mother's.

"Mom?"

Not Mom. Not Dad, either. Something else.

She peeked up to spy the loose skin at the neck. Palest blue eyes blazed down at her. The smile was thin, lined; the teeth small, stained, cramped.

Silver hair gleamed dully under the mall lights. Was this an old woman? No, it wasn't—not one like Theresa had met before. Those had never sent a frigid jolt of fear down her spine. The smell that reached Theresa's nose was unfamiliar. Years later, when she first attempted cooking, she would recognize it as something like leaking gas.

Theresa's stomach turned. She began to back up, but the hand clasping her shoulder was too strong. The specter's voice rattled from unmoving lips, thin and rasping as a winter's wind.

It said only, *"The third floor."*

Theresa wailed. She turned on her heel and smacked directly into her mother's coat. Too young to fully process why she was so frightened, let alone put it into words, she merely bleated out a pitiful cry. Likely attributing her emotional outburst to shyness at meeting Santa, her mother scooped her up and stepped quietly out of line.

If the first appearance of this figure had also been the last, Theresa may have enjoyed the Christmas season with as much mixed joy and stress as the rest of her family. Of course, it had not been the last time. Not nearly the last.

...

"Two hours—remember!" Theresa held up two fingers to further illustrate her point through the semi-frosted windshield.

Amber nodded, flashing a thumbs up before vanishing through the front door of her best friend's home.

Theresa sighed. She glanced, again, into the back seat. It was empty. Of course it was empty.

"Cut it out," she admonished herself as she pulled the car into reverse. What did she expect to see? A withered face? A ghoulish Mrs. Claus hitching a ride without invitation?

Theresa laughed, and yet her heart thumped heavily in her chest. She would like nothing more than to be home, book in one hand, hot chocolate in the other. Theresa attempted to distract herself by singing along to "Silent Night" as it crooned from the radio.

How ridiculous it was, to fear the potential glimpse of an old woman. Theresa had spent many productive hours in a therapist's chair, dissecting her terror from every angle. She eventually landed on the one theory that seemed the most logical: the mortal fear of aging. Existential dread, and nothing more.

So lost in thought was she, Theresa hadn't noticed that the Christmas song had stopped playing on the radio.

"...and remember, don't forget to visit the third floor to find the best last-second deals..."

Theresa's eyes snapped toward the radio. "What?" she asked aloud.
"...that's the third floor! It's all waiting for you on the third floor!"
Theresa's eyes flooded with tears.

"All that matters, you'll find it on the third floor! Find the truth! Find yourself! Find me waiting on the *third floor!*"

"What? No...no." Theresa reached down, began to twist the knob feverishly.

It was at this moment that a hunched figure hobbled from behind a snowbank. It stood, a black spindle on the white road.

Theresa slammed on the brakes. And all was quiet.

. . .

Once, while staring at the ceiling on a particularly sleepless night, Theresa had ranked the most unsettling of the woman's appearances.

While it was a difficult choice, it seemed the standout vision occurred while Theresa attended a movie on Christmas Eve.

Theresa was a young teenager then and determined to be as normal as possible. And she was, of course, aside from her discomfort with images of Mrs. Claus and an occasional avoidance of third floors.

Theresa and her family had decided, last second, to attend a viewing of *It's a Wonderful Life* at the local theater. Theresa smashed piles of popcorn into her face as George Bailey stared over the edge of a frozen bridge.

She had been nervous to go out. The ghastly old woman had never appeared to her at home, and as such, stepping one foot outside her front door felt like a tremendous leap every Christmas eve. She had pleaded with her family to let her skip this event, but to no avail. Still, squished between her parents and loaded with snacks, she felt safe enough for the moment.

She shouldn't have.

Five rows ahead, turned around fully in the theater chair, and half shaded in darkness, sat she—the old woman.

Theresa sucked in a sharp breath and choked on a kernel of popcorn. She wished to pull at her mother's sleeve but found herself immobilized with dread.

The phantom stared at her, boldly, unblinking. Its grizzly, lined face shone in shades of flickering gray and white as the film rolled.

Once again, the voice hissed in her ear, a frosty wind that no one else could hear: *"The third floor."*

Theresa shouted, and the woman was gone. Why could Theresa's parents not see her? Why could nobody else see her?

Was she insane, or was she being haunted?

. . .

When Theresa awoke, it took her several blinking moments to realize what had happened. She lifted her pounding head from the steering wheel and steadied her bleary vision on the road. Hadn't someone been standing on the street? If so, no longer; all she could see now were banks of snow.

Banks of snow, and one thing more. Nestled in the icy powder sat a quaint, white house with a thick sail of smoke trailing from the chimney.

Theresa turned the key in the ignition. The engine struggled, but did not turn over.

Theresa cursed and grabbed for her cell phone.

"Don't be dead, don't be dead. No, no, no. Ah!" Theresa tossed the lifeless brick to the passenger seat. How long had she been asleep for? The light looked thin and darkness loomed behind it.

She could just wait in her car. That's what she would do. Eventually someone might drive by. Right?

Theresa already knew the answer. There would be no waiting in her car. There would be no cell phone, no sudden rescue, no snow plow nor police car. She would have to go into the house.

"It's small. How many floors can it have anyway? Two, at the most. C'mon, girl, go. Go go. Don't freeze to death being a coward."

After this brief pep talk, Theresa pushed the car door open. It scraped across the rapidly piling frost. Theresa stuck one boot into the crunchy, cold ground, and then the other. She began a trudging march towards the front door.

Theresa stomped onto the porch. She peeked back once or twice to be sure that she wasn't followed by her own, personal ghost—if that's what it was, anyway.

After a puff of air and a small prayer, Theresa knocked on the door.

No one answered.

Theresa looked around. It was getting darker. She knocked again. Still, no one answered.

"Hello?" Theresa shouted, "I crashed my car in a snow drift and…I could use some help!"

Again, no one answered.

Theresa searched the horizon again. She was out in the boonies. Why did her daughter have to pick friends that lived in the middle of nowhere? Theresa's head throbbed. What else was there to do?

She didn't have a choice.

"Just do it. Do it, do it."

Theresa grabbed the doorknob. She almost wished the door were locked. It wasn't. The door opened.

"Hello?" Theresa called as she pushed her head inside. "Hello, I…" Theresa looked around carefully. To her surprise and relief, it appeared to be a perfectly normal home. "I could use some help. I'm sorry to open the door like this!"

When no one responded, Theresa pushed the door the rest of the way. She placed one foot inside.

It was just a living room. Nothing wrong here. Except…maybe, a strange smell? Even so, the house was warm and dry. Theresa was beginning to freeze. She walked inside the living room.

"Hello?" she called again.

Theresa began to look around for a phone. She took in her surroundings, from the beige shag carpet to the antique writing desk. A nice home. A little stuffy, a little dated, but someone had been taking good care of it.

But who? Where were the homeowners?

Theresa finally spotted a phone anchored to the hallway wall. Unfortunately, it was the hallway located at the top of a staircase.

Theresa grimaced as she began to gingerly climb the stairs.

"I'm not an intruder. I just, I need to use your phone for a moment, if that's okay."

As Theresa moved up the staircase, she realized what the smell was: leaking gas.

"Oh god." She stopped short. This was a mistake. She should go back. This had been wrong, wrong from the start, and she was an idiot not to have seen that. Her internal scolding session was interrupted by the shrill ring of the telephone.

Theresa yelped. She stared at the phone as it clamored on. This could mean help. This could be the way home.

Theresa thudded quickly up the remaining steps. The smell grew stronger. Even so, she tore the phone from the wall.

"Hello?" she exhaled, "My name is Theresa and I need help, my car hit a snowbank and I—"

Theresa pulled the phone back as the sound of wind hissed harshly in her ear. She stared at the receiver. She knew what would come next.

"The third floor."

Theresa yelped. She dropped the phone and twisted to run down the stairs. In a few bounds, she had reached the bottom. Theresa raced for the entryway.

There, in the darkened doorway, it stood. Its pale eyes shone grotesquely against a twilight snowscape.

"The third floor."

Theresa shrieked. She spun around again and bolted up a few steps. She paused briefly to look back. The woman was gone.

Theresa sagged against the banister to catch her breath.

"Enough," she whispered in a quivering voice. "*Okay!* I hear you…the third floor."

The only way out of this seemed to be through it.

Theresa willed her body forward. She climbed the first staircase, prepared to face her lifelong visitor. She was mildly relieved when she reached the landing without incident.

Of course, this would mean that there must be a second set of stairs.

Theresa found them too quickly...She wasn't ready. She needed time.

No. She had given this thing enough of her time. Years of it.

Theresa climbed the last flight. At the top of the staircase was a small door. It was composed of white, painted beadboard and featured a gold handle. Theresa reached out and grasped it.

"The third floor," Theresa announced as she turned the knob and peered inside.

The room was dim and silent. Two small windows framed the picturesque snowstorm as it continued to blanket the horizon. The smell of gas was strong; Theresa covered her nose with one hand.

In the center of the room was a rocking chair, its back silhouetted in the evening glow.

On that chair sat an old woman.

Theresa stood quietly for a moment. With a conviction she had never known before, she forced herself toward the chair.

"I'm...here. I'm here. It's me. Now, what...what is it that you want?"

The figure in the chair stiffened. It straightened up. It turned its head slowly toward Theresa.

After a moment, it spoke.

"What?" asked the old woman. She spoke not in a hiss, but in a clear, docile voice. "Who are you? What are you doing in my home?"

Theresa blinked. She stared at the woman. Indeed, this was the same lined faced, the same thin-lipped, iron-haired creature she had seen every year. But somehow it was different. It wasn't threatening or ghoulish. It wasn't even an 'it.'

"I..." Theresa started. "I...I don't understand, I..."

The old woman attempted to stand from her chair. Her brittle body struggled.

"If you're here to rob me, I have no money. Take what you will, but please leave me in peace."

Theresa shook her head, "No, I...no. I'm not here to rob you, I'm here...I've seen you...I've seen you every year since I was a child."

The woman stared at her. She clutched a cane in one wrinkled hand, leaned on it for support.

"I'm not sure what you're talking about. But Christmas Eve is a poor time to play a prank and harass an old woman. Please, take what you need and go." The aged woman took an unsteady step forward.

Theresa felt lightheaded. This didn't make any sense. She swayed. "No,

I…I'm not trying to…" She sniffed the air. "Wait a minute, do you smell that?"

"Smell what?" puzzled the old woman.

"That smell, that—gas. It's gas…it's a gas leak! We need to leave here."

The old woman shook her head.

"I haven't been able to smell a damn thing in ten years," she responded.

"Oh…"Theresa rubbed her forehead. "That's it, isn't it? We need to leave. That's been it the whole time. I'm meant to get you out of here!"

The old woman shrugged. "Leave to go where, dear? There is nowhere for me." She took a shambling step past Theresa. "But you should go. Go home to your family."

"No," Theresa stepped in front of the slight figure. "We have to go, it's not safe here."

The old woman lifted her face to stare into Theresa's eyes. They were pale as Theresa remembered, but mournful in a way she had never noticed before.

"Leave to go where?" The woman repeated. "As I've said, there is nowhere that I belong. Now please leave me," the old woman's voice dropped off softly.

Theresa watched her hobble by until she'd nearly reached the door. The words left Theresa's mouth before she knew that she intended to say them.

"But there is somewhere you belong. It's…with me. You've always been with me. I know it's strange, but please, trust me."

The old woman stopped. She considered Theresa.

After a long moment she smiled.

"If you say so, dear."

. . .

Forks clicked on dinner plates as Theresa and her family gobbled up the last few slices of apple pie. The old woman—named Esther, apparently— was an object of curiosity. Why had Theresa, cautious by nature, felt it right to bring home a stranger for Christmas eve dinner? And why this stranger in particular? Theresa was hesitant to mention that the gas in Esther's home would take time to clear out, even with the windows open and the valve turned off.

Esther shared her story with Theresa's family: that of her late husband, and sadly, of her late son. Away from her empty home, Esther was filled with color and warmth. Despite her appearance, she bore no actual resemblance to the being that had stalked Theresa over the years. Even Amber seemed to like her, sharing the none-too-short list of gifts she hoped to see under the tree in the morning.

"Did you remember to write and ask for some of these things?" queried

Esther.

"No," scoffed Amber, "I'm too old for that."

"I don't know," smiled Esther. "A number of years ago, when I was quite blue, I wrote a letter to you-know-who," she laughed. "I was an adult at the time, and felt silly, but my Christmas wish came true after all."

Theresa tilted her head, "What did you ask for?"

"Ah, dear, what does anyone really want for the holidays?" Esther patted Theresa's hand fondly. "For someone to give a damn about them."

Theresa squeezed Esther's hand reassuringly.

"Hm," Theresa studied her coffee as it swirled in her cup. "Huh," she said, shaking her head. "It's just…surreal."

"What is, dear?"

"I…" Theresa stared at Esther. She shook her head. "Nothing. We're just happy to have you here with us." She sighed, "I guess Santa works in mysterious ways."

A peculiar smile slipped over Esther's ancient face. "Oh no, dear. Not Santa."

"No?"

Theresa locked eyes with Esther. A wicked wind whistled outside.

"Not Santa, dear." Esther's grip tightened on Theresa's hand, steely for a woman of her age. "I wrote to Black Peter."

THE GIFT: A BIRTHDAY TALE

It sat on my table for a week. As much as I try, I can't seem to look at it for more than a few seconds.

Burgundy paper, a green bow. Square box. Polka dots. And that smell. I won't open it. I can't...no, I won't.

I've tried throwing it away. Every time I do, it just comes back. And it comes back in perfect condition. I've even tried smashing it with a baseball bat. And burying it. You would think that would have done the trick. But here it sits.

Maybe if I just go to bed. Finish my cigarette and my drink. Read a book. And go to bed. I'll know what to do with it in the morning. Things always seem better in the morning.

...

This morning I found it sitting outside of my bedroom door.

Burgundy wrapper, green bow. Square box. Polka dots. A gift tag I won't read. And...that smell.

I'll go on a long drive. Visit my sister. A few days in a hotel will do me some good. I just gotta get out of here.

I'll book a sitter for the dog. Pack my suitcase. Soon I'll be throwing one back and forgetting all about this—the smell, the box, and the name tag I will *not* read.

...

I found it again. Or, it found me. I need to think quickly. It was damn near impossible to explain why a birthday present, addressed to me, appeared on my sister's doorstep—the day before I did, no less.

She had read the tag. She just had to read that stupid, perfumed tag.

"Forever yours?" She had laughed. She actually laughed. "Good for you. I'm glad you're not letting her get you down."She shook her head. "I'm impressed though. She left you what—a month ago? And you've already found a 'forever!' I wish I could meet someone that quickly."

I grinned like an idiot and grabbed the box, shoved it in my suitcase. "Yeah, sorry… Sorry they sent it here."

She smiled at me. I love my sister, I truly do. She would never think a bad thought of her little brother. Not a really bad thought, anyway.

"It's okay. Just be careful, it looks like you're dating a detective. Now blow out your candles!"

I had taken a deep breath and given it my all.

The candles went out.

All except one.

. . .

Today is the day. It will be gone and I'll never see it again. I knew I'd built this fire pit for a reason. It has to be good for something. Time to crack open a can and enjoy the fresh air. Maybe I'll grill some hot dogs over the box as it burns.

Just to be sure, though, I'll offer up a sacrifice. I'm not sure how this all works, but I've read a few articles online and I think this could do the job.

It's a good fire, low smoke, nice dry wood.

And in it goes. Ker-plunk. Goodbye, gift!

Now, more carefully this time, I toss in the bit of brown hair I keep tied in a green ribbon. Next, a square of fabric, burgundy with polka dots. I take a quick sniff before it, too, is eaten by the flames. Lavender perfume. It's funny how smells can take you back, remind you of someone, almost like they're standing right there...wearing that polka-dot dress that looks too damn good on them.

I didn't like dragging these things up from the basement. But I gotta do what I gotta do.

There's just one problem now:

The box, it won't burn.

. . .

I woke up this morning to find the box sitting at the foot of my bed. Not a scratch on it. Not a single burn mark either.

I had locked it away in the basement last night. In a safe place.

71

I guess I don't mind it so much anymore. I can get used to anything. I had gotten used to life with her, hadn't I? Her hair on the drain, her sexy laugh, her constant accusations and suspicions. And now I'll get used to life without her.

What I can't really get used to, however, are the footprints.

The dark ones, dried muddy brown, that lead from the basement door to the foot of my bed.

...And that smell. Lavender perfume.

THE WINDOW: AN ANNIVERSARY STORY

Trisha tossed her purse onto the car floor, threw herself into the passenger seat, and howled with delight. "At long last!" She clapped her hands together and squeezed them to her chest. "I swear that time has been moving backwards these past few weeks." Trisha's husband, Dave, piled in next, pulling the door shut behind him.

"If you're excited now, wait until you see the place," he grinned at her.

Trisha took her husband's face between her hands and pulled him in for a kiss on the forehead. "You great, big, wonderful man, you. I can't believe how much work you've put in. And I really can't believe I get to see it today! *Today!*" She gave him a little shake, nearing hysteria.

"I surrender! Don't hurt me! Please!" Dave laughed, putting up both hands. He settled down and cleared his throat. "So what you're telling me is, you want me to bulldoze the new cabin and drop that dinky wooden box back in."

This earned him a slap on the arm. "Get movin', mister! Mama wants to see her new summer home!"

"Yes, ma'am!" Dave winked as he turned the key in the ignition.

During the two hour drive to the cabin, Dave and Trisha chatted excitedly over every detail of their summer plans: who to invite, and when, who not to invite, and why; the cost of their vacation home upgrade and how it would be worth every cent; and finally, how they planned to quit their jobs and exist perpetually in their new hot tub.

Trisha nearly launched from her seat like an overheated corn kernel when their new residence finally pulled into view. She gasped in pure euphoria. "Dave!" She cupped a hand to her mouth. "It's amazing!"

Where once stood a modest wooden cabin—rough at the corners, leaking here and there, but cozy enough—stood a sleek, wood-and-glass monument to her small family's hard work and good fortune. It sat nestled in a carefully curated landscape of lush pines and green grasses. The slope of the metal roof suggested Alpine lodge, but the expansive front windows promised modern luxury.

Trisha felt the sting of tears in her eyes. "It's even better than I could have imagined."

"Well, it's real, baby. And it's ours." He leaned in to kiss her cheek, "Happy anniversary, doll."

...

Trisha squeezed the phone to her ear with one shoulder, her hands occupied with unpacking. "You should see the cabinets! He sourced them from local timber. I mean, he really went all out...Why would you say that, Mom?" She dropped her bathing suit onto the bed and pulled out a pair of shorts. "Call it an apology or whatever you want to. I'm choosing to move forward. Anyway, look, I'm gonna go start dinner. Love you too...No, I'm not mad. Talk to you soon. Okay, bye, Mom."

Trisha sighed and tossed her phone down. It flopped over when it hit the mattress. She rubbed her neck. "Don't let her ruin this for you," she said as she began to walk toward the length of panoramic windows. She took a breath and reveled in the stretch of greenery that lay before her.

She heard the door open as Dave thudded in, already clad in his work boots and gloves. He wiped the sweat off his brow with the back of one hand, pulled off his cap, and swooped in for a squeeze. "Hey, baby. The view hasn't changed, but the window sure has." Dave rapped a knuckle on the floor to ceiling glass panel. "That was a pain to haul in." He looked down at her. "You know kid, my view ain't half bad either!" Dave wrapped his thick arms around Trisha and raised her an inch off the floor.

Trisha yelped. "Put me down, you big weirdo!" she squealed as she playfully batted at him.

"You got it," Dave set her down gently. "I'm going to chop the rest of that firewood. Mind grabbing my toolkit?"

"Sure," she said, "Wait—hun, where is it?" she called to his retreating form.

"In the basement!" he shouted over his shoulder.

...

"This came out great," Trisha commented as she cut into her steak.

"I aim to please," Dave replied.

Trisha took a sip of her wine. "I'm so glad that we did this. It's really...it will be good for us, I think."

Dave looked up. He nodded. A small smile stretched across his lips. He reached out for her hand. "Me too, doll. I think so too. Hey—to a fresh start." Dave raised his glass in a toast.

Trisha met his glass with hers. "To a new beginning." After another sip of wine, Trisha returned to cutting up her steak. "I just can't get over how much work you put into this. Really. Even the basement is better than the nicest room of our old cabin."

"Hey, it got the job done though, that old girl."

"It did. We had some good times there. But really, this is too much. Can you even call it a cabin anymore? Three beds, two baths—our first house was probably half this size."

Dave nodded. "I just wanted to show you how much you mean to me."

It was Trisha's turn to smile. "Hey, not to change the subject, but I meant to ask you. When I went down into the basement, there was some sort of...door? I don't know, it looked like a handle, and I went to open it, but I realized it really wasn't a door. Just a handle, I guess. In a wooden panel on the wall." Trisha chewed a bite of food. "What is that?"

"Ah, that. That opens the electrical panel. I sort of hid it away." He patted his mouth with a napkin. "Don't worry dear, that mysterious handle doesn't lead to my secret underground lair...Or does it?" He shot her a glistening grin.

"You're such a dork." Trisha stole a piece of broccoli off of his plate. "Dork tax!"

After washing the dishes, basking in front of the fire, and finishing off the wine, it was time to call it a night. Trisha and Dave brushed their teeth in tandem, changed into their pajamas, and retired to the bedroom.

Three minutes later, Trisha made her usual announcement. "I need a glass of water."

Dave chuckled, "Of course you do. Go get your water. But don't be long, sweetie."

Trisha padded out onto the cool floor. She left the bedroom, crossed the living room, and headed into the kitchen. Trisha poured herself a glass of water and took a few deep gulps. She turned and set her glass down on the counter. And then she screamed.

The light was pale blue as it poured in from the windows. All was as it should be: the fat moon, the glimmering map of stars, the dense rope of trees. But there, in the middle of this serenity, stood a figure. No, not just a figure. Pressed against the glass, palms flat to the translucent panes, stood the backlit silhouette of a man.

"D-Dave!" Trisha shouted as she gasped for breath. "Dave! Come here!"

Her husband pounded out like an oncoming storm.

"What? What is it?"

Trisha aimed a shaking arm at the window. "It's—it's, it's—a man! There's someone out there!"

75

Dave rushed to turn on the light. He pounded to the window and cupped his hands around his eyes. "Where, honey?"

Trisha clutched at her chest. "He was there, I saw him."

Dave flicked on the perimeter light. "Babe, I don't see anything."

Trisha trembled as tears rushed to her eyes. "But he was there. And I don't think…I don't think he was wearing any clothes."

Trisha didn't care for the way her husband examined her. "Okay, Trish. I think your eyes are playing tricks on you." He approached, arms out. "Hey, if someone was out there, the alarm would have gone off. And it didn't, right? Hey…" Dave gathered his wife into his arms. "It's nothing, doll."

Trisha initially pulled away, but eventually fell into his embrace. Her eyes remained glued to the window.

…

"Morning, babe." Trisha jumped, splashing coffee onto the counter. "Oh—sorry!" Dave apologized, "Still spooked, huh?"

Trisha shook her head. "You would be, too."

Dave accepted the coffee she offered. "Thanks. Ooh, hot!" He blew on the steaming cup. "I'm sure I would be! Sounds scary. But you know, the way the light reflects off the trees around here, I'm sure it could look like anything."

Trisha's brows soared. "Light reflecting off of trees? You think I could mistake a reflection of bushes and grass for a naked man?"

"I don't know. Maybe. Depends on how hairy the guy is. But the next time you're desperate to see a naked man, do me a favor and let me know."

Trisha stared at her husband, hard. He waggled his eyebrows. Finally, she smiled.

"I hate you." She tossed a dish towel at his head.

"Hate you, too. Now get your bathing suit on. We're going kayaking!"

…

"Well I know what you think about it, Mom, but the therapist said this could be a good chance to reconnect." Trisha polished a glass to clear perfection. "Mm-hm. No…" Trisha's voice dropped. "I know for sure that he doesn't talk to her anymore. He hasn't since—you know what, Mom, I'm not up for discussing this. I just wanted to let you know that things are going great here, and we're happy, and everything is fine, so…" She placed the glass in a cabinet. "I know you do. I love you too. Okay. I'll call you tomorrow. Goodnight, Mom."

"Hey doll—you coming to bed?" Dave's voice echoed from the bedroom.

"Coming!" Trisha did a quick wipe of the counter before hanging the hand towel on its bar.

Trisha switched off the light and shuffled across the floor as quickly as she could. She covered the side of her face with one hand to avoid looking at the massive window.

In an instant, she felt her phone slip from her hand and fall to the floor. Her stomach sank as she heard the sharp *crack* that meant irreparable damage.

Cursing, Trisha spun around to gather the remains of her only-three-month-old cell phone. "Nooo," she groaned as she knelt down to inspect the damage.

When she lifted her eyes, they landed on two bodies pressed against the window.

Trisha sucked in air as she fell backwards. She began to scramble wildly away from the clear barrier, the only thing that protected her from these unwelcome visitors. The man was back. Difficult as it was to discern detail, Trisha felt certain it was the same silhouette. But this time he was joined by a smaller figure: a female. And as with the first appearance, they were both nude. The pallid bodies held their hands against the glass. She could not make out their faces.

"Dave!" Trisha wailed.

"What...hun, what is it?"

Trisha backed away until she hit the wall. Her gaze never left the figures. "DAVE!"

Her husband's heavy footfalls echoed down the hall. "Hun, what is it?"

The light flicked on, and they were gone.

Trisha burst into tears. "I want to get out of here. I want to go home."

Dave blinked at her. "Trish...Oh honey, your phone."

Trisha scrambled up the wall, "I don't *care* about my phone. I care about the people shoving their hideous bodies against our windows. I care about leaving here alive—and sane."

Dave walked to the window, peered out into the yard. "What, you thought you saw someone out there again?"

"No, Dave, I don't *think* I saw anything. *I saw someone.* Two people!"

Her husband scanned the perimeter. He sighed. "I mean, I believe you, sweetie. But there is no one out there. How could they be there one second, and be gone the next?"

"I don't know!" Trisha shouted. "And I don't care! I want to leave!"

Dave approached arms open for an embrace. Trisha shoved him away. "No!" she barked. "We need to leave now!"

Another sigh. Dave rubbed the back of his neck. "Look, honestly, I think I know what's going on here."

"You...you do?" Trisha felt the need to brace herself.

"I do." Dave was silent for a moment. "I think that whether you know it or not, you weren't ready for this trip. You still haven't forgiven me." He lifted a hand to silence her. "Wait, wait. You thought you were past it. But you aren't. And you know, part of me understands that, hun. But another part of me feels like you're trying to sabotage this whole thing."

Trisha's jaw could have hit the floor. "Sabotage? Really? Is that what you think?"

Dave crossed his arms, jaw set. "I do. I know you're not intending to, but that is exactly what you're doing."

"I..." Trisha could only shake her head. "I don't even know what to say to that."

Her husband crossed the room, reached for her hands. "Say you'll stay, sweetie. Say you'll try. I've worked so hard on this place. And these things you think you're seeing...Isn't there any chance, any at all, that you're seeing them as a way to end our trip early?"

Trisha could only stare at Dave.

"Look," he went on, "I'll check the yard. I'll make sure everything is fine. Then we'll start a fire and cuddle up with some wine. Okay?"

Trisha looked down at the floor. "I..."

He squeezed her hands tighter. "One more day, honey. Give this a chance. I was finally starting to feel like things were...normal between us."

Trisha blew out a breath from her nose. "One more day."

"And if those imaginary weirdos show up again, I'll punch them to the moon."

Trisha cracked a smirk. "Alright, Slugger."

...

Trisha poked futilely at the carcass of her phone. "You klutz," she chastised herself. The most she had been able to prod from it was a flickering white screen.

"You just won't give up on it, huh?" Dave was steadily chopping vegetables in the kitchen.

"I guess not..." she replied.

"Just call it. Time of death, 5:04 pm."

Trisha smiled despite herself. "Okay. Maybe I'll bury it in the backyard."

"Sounds good. Actually babe, while you're out there, mind grabbing my wood gloves? I think I left them outside somewhere."

"And you need them...now?" Trisha glanced his way. Dave was elbow deep in zucchini skins.

"I don't want them to get rained on." He said imploringly, "They're my good pair."

"Okay then." Trisha stood up, slipped on her shoes and began to head outside.

"Babe?" Dave held up a finger to pause her. "If you can't find them, I might have left them in the shed."

"Okay, honey." Trisha reached for the door handle.

"Or on the deck!" he called again.

Trisha was halfway through the door as she replied, "I'll look, sweetie."

"Or on the woodblock—!"

"Dave!" she hissed as she slipped onto the soft grass.

Trisha walked the perimeter of the yard, taking the opportunity to stretch her legs. In the light of day, she did feel lucky to be here. Trisha listened to the melodic cacophony of the birds. She inhaled the fresh scent of pine and woodsmoke.

Trisha crossed the lawn and headed for the shed. She scanned the grass, the work bench, and the cutting stump for her husband's gloves. When the obvious places were searched, she took hold of the shed door and pushed it open.

Trisha stepped inside. She batted a cobweb out of her face. For all the work he did on the cabin, Dave had never bothered to replace this ramshackle little box of a building.

"Aha," she announced as she spotted them. Trisha closed the few feet to the worktable and snapped up the gloves. She turned to head out when something caught her eye.

Balled in the corner, like a sheer tumbleweed, was what appeared to be a set of nylon pantyhose. But...it couldn't be. Trisha herself never wore them; she found even the silkiest pair to be too itchy. Trisha approached the little bundle. She reached down and scooped it up.

She unfurled the underwear in her arms like a limp snake. They were pantyhose, no mistake about that. There were a number of tears and holes in the soft fabric. She followed one leg down to the foot, where she found a dull maroon stain. It was...

Trisha tossed the pantyhose down to the ground. Her heart hammered in her chest. It couldn't be. But it was.

It was blood.

Trisha balled the pantyhose up how she found it. She placed it carefully back in the corner of the shed, exited the small structure, and began to walk toward the house. She stopped in the yard, watching her husband through the substantial window.

There he stood, dicing away. Had she never really noticed how imposing he was? How powerful? How cunningly charming? Hadn't he always been adept at keeping secrets?

And then there was that strange door handle to nowhere—the one in the basement.

"No. No, stop that." She shook her head. There was no room for such thoughts. Isn't this just what Dave had been accusing her of? Was she actually trying to sabotage their chance at a fresh start?

Trisha gathered her nerves and started toward the door. She was sure that there was some kind of reasonable explanation.

If only she could think of one.

...

"Honey?"

"Mm-hm?" Dave replied through a mouth full of food.

"You know I was thinking, you might not always be around when I'm here. Wouldn't it be a good idea to show me how to flip the breaker?"

"What's that, sweetie?"

"The breaker. You said the handle downstairs was to the electrical panel, but I couldn't seem to open it. Maybe after dinner you could show me how?"

Dave's chewing slowed. She watched the line of his jaw, hard and tight with muscle, move under his skin. He glanced up and appeared to consider her for a moment.

"Where's this coming from? You've never worried about this kind of thing before."

Trisha forced a smile. "Oh you know, with the way my mind's been playing tricks on me lately...I just wouldn't want to get stuck here in the dark!"

Dave leaned back. The chair creaked beneath his weight.

Finally, he spoke.

"But why would I ever leave you alone here, doll?"

...

Trisha lay in bed, body stiff, eyes glued to the ceiling.

She had to come up with a plan. She had to find a way out of here.

Dave snored softly next to her. In an unprecedented act, he had placed his cell phone under his pillow as he slept.

There would be only one way out: she would need to get up, unnoticed, find the keys, and make it to the car.

Easy enough, except for the bodies that would be pressed horribly against the window, waiting for her.

But that could be ignored. It would have to be. She wasn't sure that the figures were real in the first place; Dave could be right, after all. But maybe they weren't meant as a disruption. Maybe her mind had conjured them as a warning.

There was no time like the present. Trisha carefully lifted one foot. She began to push up and out of bed.

Trisha nearly lost her nerve when Dave's breath caught mid-snore. She stilled. After a moment, his breathing returned. She kept going.

Trisha tip-toed toward the door. Thankfully, mercifully, Dave had left the keys on the dresser. It must have escaped his notice. Trisha pinched them between two fingers, praying that they were silent as she lifted them. They were, and she squeezed them to her palm.

Trisha padded silently out of the room. She turned the corner and crept down the hall. When she reached the end, she stopped.

They were going to be there. She knew it. She was going to see them. But there was no reason to believe they were real. If she could just make it to the car, she would be on the road and headed straight for the police station.

Trisha drew in a breath. She counted down in her head.

3…2…1…

With all the bravery she could muster, Trisha raced for the door.

She couldn't help herself. She had to look.

And there they were. There were three this time. One man, two women. She saw the whites of their palms as they leaned into the glass. Their faces were hidden in darkness, but she thought she caught the glint of their eyes.

Trisha fought back a scream. She dropped her gaze to the floor and kept running. When she was a few short feet from the door, she looked up again.

There were four now. Another man had joined them. They all stood, still as the night, with the exception of their heads, which were now turned toward her. With a sinking feeling, Trisha realized they were tracking her. Trisha fought back tears as she grabbed for the handle.

She missed. She looked down, grasped it firmly. Her vision swerved back, frantically, to the window. Five. There were five now. This new one was smaller, perhaps a child or teenager. They formed a ghastly row: shoulder to shoulder, they were a wall of fleshy bodies, and a barrier to Trisha's escape.

Trisha ripped the door open. In her calculations, she had forgotten one thing: the alarm.

The high pitched beep started immediately. Trisha scrambled to punch in the code.

5-2-4-7-7…no, wait, that was the old code.

Trisha began to wheeze. Her eyes were drawn irresistibly to the window. Another had joined. A woman. Was it six, seven now? She could barely see straight.

5-2-1-4…was it four or seven that came next? What had he told her?

Too late. The alarm went off.

"No…" Trisha dropped her head. She covered her ears with her hands.

Trisha's husband emerged from the shadows of the hall. He stood, fists balled, face taught.

"What do you think you're doing, doll?"

Trisha looked up at him. "Please…" she implored. "Please, I just want to go home."

Out of the corner of her eye, another had appeared. But Dave wasn't looking at them.

"Please, baby, we can talk later," Trisha begged. "I just want to leave."

Her husband stalked closer. "You know what, Trish? That's the problem with us, isn't it? You never really trusted me. From day one, you were ready to throw in the towel as soon as things got hard."

"No, no," she sobbed. "No, honey, that's not it. I just want to go home, and—and—" she gagged on the air. Another had appeared.

Only now they were all watching Dave.

"And what? We'll go home and you'll forgive me?" Another step closer.

"Yes, baby, I will—"

"We'll go home and it will be like none of it ever happened? Is that it, sweetheart?"

"Yes, I promise, I—"

"And let me guess. We'll go home, and you'll touch me again?" His voice broke. "Love me again?"

Trisha trembled. She stared at him. Her mouth opened and closed.

"That's what I thought. No, hun. I don't think so. You're not taking the easy way out. You're staying right here."

He was close now. Too close. Trisha peeked at the window.

The length of the glass was now filled with dark figures. They pressed their hands eagerly against it, tracking her husband like starving dogs.

Trisha shook her head. "You...can't see them."

Dave scoffed. "See what? Your invisible friends? Honey, no offense, but sometimes I think you need help."

"You're right," she agreed quietly. "I think I do..." *Just not* that *kind,* thought Trisha.

She frantically searched the immediate area for something to grab. She spotted it quickly enough: Dave's wood cutting axe, which he left propped against the wall.

Dave followed his wife's line of sight. In an instant, he lunged for the axe.

Trisha was quicker. She grabbed the handle and hurled herself toward the window. She threw the axe at the glass with every ounce of strength she could summon.

The pane exploded into a million shards. It rained down like clear sand, spraying into the yard and showering the motionless bodies. Trisha felt a few sharp pieces of glass assault the exposed flesh of her arms and legs.

There the bodies stood, wordless and unmoving. Every face was turned toward her. She could really see them now. Some were bloated. Others were gouged, cut, and bruised. One was deteriorated to the skull, with only strips of flesh and fine tufts of hair clinging to the bone like cobwebs.

But none of them came for her.

"What the hell is wrong with you!" Dave bellowed.

Trisha's eyes left the bodies and landed on her husband. He was sweating. The veins in his arms bulged.

"There *is* something wrong with me," she replied. "I put my trust in the wrong people...Goodbye, Dave."

Without another moment's delay, Trisha bolted to the car.

She pounded across the wet grass, unlocking the door as she flew. Trisha did not stop to observe the figures.

Somehow, she knew. She understood now. They weren't here for her. They never were.

Trisha grabbed the handle, ripped the door open, and hurtled into the car. She slammed the door shut and locked it. As she started the vehicle, she allowed herself a glance at the gruesome bodies.

They all had turned their heads to look back at her. Then, slowly, they faced forward again.

The first stepped across the glassy threshold and entered the house. Then the second. Then the third, and so on, until all of the figures had stepped into the cabin.

She watched Dave, who had been making for the front door, suddenly come to a halt.

Trisha threw the car in reverse. She pressed on the gas.

She didn't want to watch what happened next

THE PARTY: A GRADUATION TALE

"When I say 6:30, I don't mean 6:45, Liz."

"What's the big deal, Dad? It's a family party. They'll expect us to be late."

Kevin shook his head. "I don't know where you learned this. I'm always on time."

"Let's blame it on Mom then." Elizabeth staggered forward, her heel stuck in the soft lawn. "Awesome. I've damaged their perfect yard."

Kevin turned back and took his daughter by the elbow to assist her. She pulled her foot from her shoe and bent down to wrench it free.

"Who needs a yard this big, anyway? Or a house this massive?" She popped the shoe back onto her foot. "Does our family have money that I don't know about?"

"If they do, I wish they'd let me in on the secret." Kevin looked up at the house on the hill. It was stunning in an understated, we-don't-want-to-show-off sort of way. "Your uncle Frank has done well for himself."

"Is that a nice way of saying that he married Aunt Charlotte for her fat bank account?"

Sure that his daughter was steady, Kevin dropped his hand. He studied her for a moment. Tall and statuesque as his ex-wife, with smooth copper hair and big hazel eyes, she was every bit as beautiful as her mother—and twice as judgmental.

"Do you think we could manage a nice, friendly visit tonight? Your cousin only graduates college once."

Liz snorted. "And since it's Glenn, I'm surprised it's happening at all."

"Alright, okay, get it out of your system now." He took a breath of cool evening air. It was a crisp night, with just a hint of sun left on the horizon.

"I can't help it," she went on. "They're just so full of themselves. Who has a cocktail party, in full formal wear, for their *graduation*? My party was

85

burgers on the grill, a cookie tray and balloons in the backyard."

"Yes, I remember," Kevin sighed. "To be fair, that was only high school." Liz shot him an annoyed glance. "Can't we just go in, say hello, make small talk, and leave without insult or incident?" He offered a smile. "We can go for ice cream after."

"Gee golly, Pop," Liz mocked as she started up the hill again. "That hasn't worked since I was eight."

"Ten years too late then. Guess I'll eat all the ice cream myself."

Liz smiled. "Just leave me a tub of rocky road and a spoon. The rest is yours."

"Deal." Kevin placed a hand on the small of her back as she continued to traverse the small hill. They cut across the grass to reach the paved walkway. Kevin took an agile step to dodge a few chalk drawings on the cement. "Oh, look at that."

Liz looked down. "Nice artwork. I think I see…is that an eye? Next to some kind of deformed bird."

Kevin tilted his head. "And a person sitting on a chair."

"I feel like when I was a kid, I stuck with rainbows and butterflies," critiqued Liz.

"Yeah, you did. But then you weren't the daughter of a prestigious museum curator, were you?"

"Nope. And that's why I'm going to a state school." Elizabeth flashed a toothy smile at her father.

"Beggars can't be choosers," Kevin mumbled under his breath.

When they reached the door, Kevin plucked the big brass knocker off its rest and delivered three hard raps.

They waited for what felt like a small eternity. Liz began to look around.

Kevin reached out and knocked on the door once more. Again, nothing happened.

"Are we…? Is this the wrong night?"

"No, I'm sure the invitation said tonight…" Kevin patted his pockets. "Damn."

"Don't have it, do you, Dad?"

"No, but—"

The door swung abruptly open.

A woman stood before them, sparkling in a sequined gold and black gown. She was older—the phrase *well preserved* came to mind—and attractive, with carefully arranged silver hair and brown, almond-shaped eyes.

"Why…hello!" The woman looked between Kevin and his daughter. "And how is it that I may help you this evening?"

Kevin fought the urge to take a step back and check the number on the mailbox. This was the right house, wasn't it?

"Uh, hi…yes, we're here for the party. It is tonight, isn't it?"

The woman considered them for longer than felt necessary. "So it is," she replied softly. "Would you indulge me by providing your invitation?"

Kevin thought he heard the trace of an accent in her voice. But if it was ever there, it had long since faded.

"My invitation? I didn't think to bring it."

"You didn't? How unfortunate," she purred.

Liz cut in, razor-tongued, "Listen, ma'am, I'm not trying to be rude here,but when exactly did my uncle hire a bouncer?"

Something in the woman's face seemed to shift. She raised one perfectly drawn eyebrow. "Ah. You're family."

"We are. So will you step aside and let us celebrate with my cousin, or do we have to slip you a twenty first?"

"Elizabeth!" Kevin gasped.

"Bribes won't be necessary. Please, come inside," a smile slithered onto the woman's face as she stepped back and opened the door.

Kevin looked at his daughter. He grappled with a sense of unease which he could not explain. He peeked inside briefly before waving an arm in front of him, "After you."

As they entered the home, they were hit with a wall of scent. Kevin took a whiff and waved it away. "Whoo! Is someone smoking?"

His daughter pinched his arm. "That's incense, Dad," she whispered. "*Now* who's being rude?"

Kevin looked around the formal living room. It was filled with people and had a party atmosphere, to be sure. He scanned for a familiar face. "Let me know if you see Frank or Glenn, will you?"

"I'll let you know if I see anyone under one-hundred-and-fifty years old, how about that?" she shot back.

Kevin waded through the room, feeling awkward and underdressed. He reached back instinctively for his daughter's arm.

"Stop," she hissed, "they'll think I'm your date."

Kevin recoiled his hand. The room had a hazy, sultry quality he had never encountered here before this visit. New decor featuring carved statues of baboons and tall, leafy plants seemed to be novel additions as well. Soft instrumental music played in the background.

In this vaguely alien environment, it was almost surreal to hear a familiar voice. "Kevin? Kevin, is it?"

Kevin turned on his heel to face a tall, bookish man with a long nose and thinning gray hair. He spoke in a pristine English accent.

"Your name is Kevin, if I'm not mistaken?" asked the gentleman.

"Yes, it's...I'm Kevin, yes." He stared at the man, trying to place him. It finally hit him. "You're my brother's boss, aren't you? The director of the museum? Mr. Harris?"

The man chuckled and bowed his head forward. "Myself, and none other." He lifted his head. "I wasn't aware that you would be attending tonight's gathering. I'm quite surprised to see you, if I'm to be honest!" His tone was light, polite, and slightly accusatory.

Kevin didn't care for it. "Why wouldn't I be here? It's my nephew's party."

The gentleman simply smiled. After a moment he spoke, "Indeed it is." He took a breath. "Well, you're here now, aren't you?"

"Looks like it," fired Elizabeth. "So where should we put Glenn's card?"

Mr. Harris stepped forward and offered his palm. "I'd be delighted to deliver that for you." As she handed him the envelope, another voice piped up from behind them.

"Liz? *Kevin?*" Frank slowly approached, his bald head gleaming in the golden lamplight.

"Uncle Frank! There you are! We were starting to get worried we were at the wrong house." Liz served up one of her most genuine smiles. In Kevin's observation, she looked slightly relieved.

Frank looked back and forth between them. "What are—"

"They've come to attend the festivities, of course!" interjected Mr. Harris. "They wish to celebrate young Glenn's graduation." He clasped his hands together. "As we all are."

"Er...yes, Frank, that's right." Kevin offered his brother his hand. "Good to see you. It's been a while, hasn't it?"

Frank reached out, slowly, and grasped his brother's hand. He began to mechanically move it up and down. "It has been." Kevin felt his brother's grip tighten beyond comfort or normalcy. He was ready to comment on this when Frank suddenly dropped his hand.

"How terribly rude we've been. Can we offer you a drink?" asked Mr. Harris.

"Absolutely!" chimed Liz, finally pleased.

"Right this way, my lovely girl," the stately man led Elizabeth toward the antique bar.

Kevin watched them retreat before turning to make small talk with his brother. "So, Frank, is Glenn excited about graduating?"

Frank stared at his brother. He reached into his jacket and produced a silken handkerchief. He began to towel off his domed forehead. "What? Uh, yes, he is."

Kevin nodded. "Okay. Good. Does he have exciting plans for the sum—"

"Look, Kev," Frank leaned in confidentially. "The invitation said next week. Next Saturday evening. Not tonight."

Kevin's brows furrowed. "I don't understand."

"The party is next weekend, Kevin."

Kevin gestured around. "So what is this if not a party?"

"Kevin, listen to me—"

Without warning, the sparkling woman they had encountered at the door slinked up to Frank's arm.

"Frank! I wasn't even aware that you had a brother. I'm afraid I made rather a poor impression of myself upon his arrival."

Frank squeezed his eyes shut. He stepped back away from Kevin and took a breath. "Kevin, may I introduce you to Mrs. Akila Davies?"

The woman produced a gloved hand for Kevin's admiration.

Kevin took the woman's hand with uncertainty. After a self-conscious pause, he pressed it to his lips. "I'm...very pleased to meet you."

"How awfully polite of you, after the way I acted. You must think me a true villain."

"No, not at all," replied Kevin, "I just didn't realize my nephew's party was so exclusive. Where is Glenn anyway?"

"Oh, he'll be along," the woman replied breezily.

"Okay..." Kevin cleared his throat. A bizarre silence stretched between them. "Frank, mind if I use the bathroom?" *'Why am I asking permission?'* Kevin wondered. Hadn't he used it a dozen times before?

"Yes. Of course. Why don't I show you where it is?" Frank made to step forward, but the stately creature at his side held tight.

"Actually, Frank, my dear, I was wondering if I could have a word with you?" The manner in which Mrs. Akila Davies made this request left little room for denial. Frank looked down at her and back up at his brother, a hint of alarm in his gaze.

"No worries, Frank, I know where to go." Kevin was only too happy for an opportunity to escape this uncomfortable interaction. He turned and slipped back into the small crowd, ducking and weaving as he made his way to the restroom.

As he ventured forward, a few pairs of eyes strayed in his direction. He spotted his daughter near the bar, sipping some kind of wine, still chatting with the distinguished Mr. Harris. The nearest bathroom was just down the hall. Perhaps he would use it and then see if Elizabeth also wanted to make it a very early night.

Kevin was almost to the bathroom when he noticed a stream of light pouring from the second to last door. It sent an amber beam across the otherwise shadowed, hardwood floor. Kevin slowed down. He lingered in front of the cracked door, hesitant to pass.

Soft voices sounded from within the room. They were speaking in unison. Kevin leaned closer, straining to hear what was being said. He could tell easily enough that they were not speaking in English—nor Spanish, nor French or German for that matter. Whatever it was, they were chanting it carefully, slowly:

"...ān nek... Tahuti Maāt... ment rā neb χeft - k ertāu en set..."

Kevin tucked against the wall. He tilted over just enough to peek in, as the chanting continued.

"...*Sebàu χer... āāui - fqaus...*"

Kevin was able to glimpse a pair of raised hands, palms turned up, bent at the elbows. The arms were set low; the person must have been kneeling.

"...*nahem en Rā ret - f...*"

Kevin dared to lean an inch further. He saw movement. A long shadow crossed the wall, like a slender hook or a gently curved talon.

Kevin squinted, trying to make out the shape of the thing that would cast such a shadow.

He wouldn't have to guess for long. Without further warning, a lengthy, needle-thin black beak pierced the slice of light emitting from the small opening.

Kevin's breath caught in his throat. He pulled back from the doorway and pressed against the wall. The chanting had stopped. He waited for the door to open, to be discovered and questioned. With great discomfort, Kevin realized that he wasn't sure that questioning was the worst of what he was about to face.

A few moments passed. Nothing happened. Then, slowly, the door creaked open. A woman stepped into the hallway. She, too, was wearing a gold and black gown. Kevin was both confused and struck by her beauty. With smooth skin, an oval face and eyes of deepest brown, she reminded Kevin of an old Hollywood starlet from some exotic picture.

She spoke in a voice equally as alluring. "May I help you?"

Kevin's mouth opened and shut like a fish. With some effort, he gathered his voice, "Um, yes, I...I was just...looking for the restroom."

The woman lifted a slender arm. She gestured behind her. "I believe what you're looking for is just ahead."

"Yes... yes, thank you." Kevin shuffled forward. As he went, he couldn't help but steal a glimpse into the room.

He couldn't be sure, but he thought he spotted a row of kneeling figures, their backs toward the door.

...

Crouched over the bathroom sink, Kevin splashed some cold water on his face. He reached for the hand towel and pressed it to his eyes. "What the actual..." Kevin stood up and blinked at his reflection. "Just calm down and get some air."

Kevin made a swift exit from the bathroom. He glanced around carefully. Sure that no one would notice him, he proceeded to his brother's home office. Kevin stepped inside and quietly shut the door behind him. A pair of french doors stood on the opposite wall, offering a view of the well manicured courtyard just beyond.

Kevin crossed the room and stepped outside. The air had already gotten cooler since he arrived at the party. Kevin let it fill his lungs. He fumbled around for his cell phone, checking that he had signal. *"Thanks for the drink, Frank, but I've got to get Liz back to her mother,"* he practiced aloud. *"No, thank you, we did our bloodletting before we left the house. We'll pass this time…"* Despite his nerves, Kevin chuckled.

Kevin had turned on his heel to enter the house when he heard an odd noise.

It was coming from the garden. And there it was again. It was soft, pleading. Kevin shook his head. "Don't go looking for trouble," he told himself. He readied to walk inside.

But there it was again.

Kevin cursed as he crossed the yard and crept toward the garden. The rear light only dimly illuminated the artfully landscaped grounds. Kevin jumped as a tangle of vines brushed his leg.

There it was. "Oh, no…" Kevin saw a rope tied to the base of a large fountain. He stepped around it and his suspicions were confirmed. Tied helplessly to the stone structure was a small brown and white goat.

"What the hell is this?" Kevin's mind spun in every direction. He tugged at his hair. *This can't be what I think it is.*

Again, the pitiful creature bleated. Kevin approached slowly, hands up. "Okay, little guy," he soothed, "you're all right now." As he stepped forward, the goat inched away. "Shhh," he reached out and stroked its ear. "What on earth are you doing here?"

Kevin knelt down next to it. The goat began to gently nibble his clothes. He sighed. "Listen. I don't know what they've got planned for you, but I'm not sticking around to see it." He glanced back at the house, at the amber light glowing in the windows.

"And you won't either." Fearing that he'd gone quite mad, Kevin untied the poor animal. "Go on, go!" He shooed the creature away. The goat began to wander off, in search of food or freedom. Kevin hoped he found both.

…

The party had a vibrant energy when Kevin returned; at every corner, there was the din of chatter, the clinking of drinks or a chorus of laughter. He threaded his way through the group, scanning eagerly for his daughter.

After several minutes, Kevin began to feel desperate. "Liz!" he hissed through the crowd. "Liz! Elizabeth—excuse me miss, sorry—Liz! Where are you?"

The party-goers occasionally stopped to spare him a glance. Kevin spotted Mrs. Davies, and crossed quickly to her. "Mrs. Davies, please, a word?"

The woman nodded at him, "Of course. Are you enjoying the party?"

"Yes, I am—it's great. Have you seen Liz?"

She sipped her drink. "Liz?"

"My daughter, Elizabeth."

"Ah, yes. Beautiful girl, isn't she?"

Kevin was growing impatient. "Thank you, she is…But have you seen her? I can't seem to find her anywhere."

Mrs. Davies swirled her drink in its glass. "I can't recall that I have. The last I saw her, she was deep in conversation with Mr. Harris." Another sip. "I believe he's rather taken with her. Perhaps he sees something special in your daughter."

Kevin's heart pumped faster. "Well, that's very nice, but…I really need to find her. If you could help me, I'd like to take her home."

"Home already?" Mrs. Davies laughed, "Why in heavens would you leave now? Glenn's graduation is about to begin!"

"Glenn's…what? His ceremony isn't for two more weeks."

A coy smile stretched across the woman's plum-colored lips.

"As you said yourself, my dear…You came to celebrate your nephew's passage to the next stage of his life. And why wouldn't you? You are family, after all."

Kevin took a step back. He turned, shouldering his way through heavily perfumed bodies. "Liz!" he barked.

Without warning, a hush fell over the room.

Kevin spun around. The music had stopped.

A single, deep, melodic voice stretched through the thick air.

"*Tua Rā… χeft uben - f …em χut ābtet ent pet…*"

The crowd slowly parted, allowing the singing figure to pass through it. The man continued his wail as he walked. In his hands, he cradled a golden scroll.

Each person the man passed dropped silently to their knees. It was not long before Kevin was the only one standing. No one looked at him, their eyes all trained to the floor.

No one, that was, except his brother. Frank was kneeling on the other side of the room. He caught Kevin's stare for an instant, before lowering his gaze. Kevin was horrified to recognize the look on his brother's face: it was, unmistakably, shame.

Feverishly, helplessly, Kevin sank to his knees to join the others.

The man at the center of the room began to orate again. Kevin was surprised when he spoke in English.

"Today we offer praise, for our family grows."

At this, the crowd chanted back, their breath rushing from their throats: *Haa! Haa!*

"This young man's journey does not end today, nor does it begin. It continues." The robed man lifted his arm.

"*Haa! Haa!*"

From behind him, a drum began to sound in a steady rhythm. Kevin fought the urge to jump to his feet, fists at the ready. Just then, Kevin noticed movement in the hallway. He watched his nephew, clad in a gold robe and ornate headdress, emerge from the shadows.

Glenn walked into the middle of the circle. He turned to face the orator.

"*Haa! Haa!*" they hissed.

Glenn's voice was whisper-soft, almost timid. "It is only through sacrifice that we may transcend to the next stage of our being."

"*Haa! Haa!*"

Kevin's chest tightened. He scanned the crowd ever more fervently for his daughter.

"It is so," responded the robed man. "However, it would appear our sacrifice was unworthy for offering for it has vanished in accordance to a will greater than ours."

Kevin bit his cheek. *The goat.*

The robed figure unfurled the scroll. He began his melodic chant once again.

A procession of women began to pour from the darkened hall. In them, Kevin recognized the beautiful woman he had encountered earlier that evening.

He also recognized his daughter.

Elizabeth floated across the floor, her steps light on her bare feet. She had a dazed, serene expression, as if staring into the stars. She, too, now wore a glimmering gown of gold. She held a silky, powder blue pillow—and on it, gleamed a spiral dagger.

"No!" Kevin barked. He began to rise to his feet.

"*Haa! Haa!*" the guests huffed again.

Kevin launched forward, his finger aimed at the master of ceremonies. "That is my daughter and you will not touch her. Do you hear me?"

"*Haa! Haa!*" The chants took on a taunting quality.

"Stop it. Stop that!" He turned to face the kneeling group. "Whatever is going on here, whatever you're doing, it's none of my business. I'm sorry. I'm sorry that we interrupted. But my daughter and I will go now. If no one interferes, we swear—we swear on our lives—we won't speak a word of this to anyone."

"*Haa! Haa!*"

The orator began to chant again.

"*...ānet' hrā-k ... χu Θā...*"

Kevin grabbed his daughter's elbow. "Liz, let's go." He tugged her forward.

His daughter took an unsteady step, and then stopped. She stood still, rooted to the floor.

Kevin spun back and looked into his daughter's eyes. They were darker than he remembered. He leaned in and whispered, imploringly, "Honey, we have to go. Do you realize what this is? Do you know what they're going to do to you?”

Elizabeth blinked. She looked up at him.

She smiled.

“No, Dad. Not me. I am destined for transcendence."

“Wha…what?” His grip loosened on her arm.

“They’re offering me a chance for more...A chance at a better life.”

“Liz…” Kevin shook his head. “Please. You're not making sense. We have to go!”

“Daddy…”

“*Haa! Haa!*” The drum beat louder.

“Elizabeth, now!” He pleaded.

His daughter gazed at him lovingly. “You always wanted what’s best for me.”

“*Haa! Haa!*”

Her hand wrapped around the dagger.

Kevin staggered backwards. His eyes filled with tears. "Elizabeth..."

“I promise,” she said solemnly. "I’ll never forget your sacrifice.”

ABOUT THE AUTHOR

Jolene Wightman is a lifelong devotee of all things horror. Though this is her first publication, her unofficial start in the world of spooky writing came in the form of pen-pal letters sent to the ghost residing in the abandoned mansion next to her childhood home. She lives in beautiful central Pennsylvania with her dog, Harmon, and her bunnies, Puff and Pippa. Though she is a social worker by day, Jolene is also a prominent member of a local horror movie club and plays the banjolele in a small folk group.